BLACK HONEY™

and other unsavory things

written by

STEVE VAN SAMSON

with art by Derek Rook

For Christine
(my amazing wife not the evil car)

FOREWARD & ACKNOWLEDGMENTS

The book represents a smattering of lovingly crafted nightmares that I've written over the last five years. While some were published previously and others are making their debut, you'll be hard pressed to find a happy ending in the bunch. Regarding the presentation, Rough House Publishing has knocked it out of the park again with a heap of new collectibles featuring art by myself and Derek Rook!

~Steve Van Samson

BLACK
HONEY

Black Honey

The carriage lumbered down the dusty, leaf-laden road with no particular urgency. Along with the steady grinding of wheels, a lone night bird called up to the stars. But behind these was another sound.

The humming was subtle at first–dismissible. It was a sound the driver hadn't heard in a very long time. Hearing it now caused a phantom mass, colder than the air, to harden in his lungs. The sound spoke to the driver–accusing him of things he no longer had strength to deny. Back in Albany, he had tried to convince his two prospective passengers to let him take the long way to their eventual destination in New Haven, Connecticut. Unfortunately, the couple were the most insufferable sort of young people–students.

The woman seemed quiet and bookish but friendly enough. She didn't oppose the extra day on the road... at least, not until her beau did. When the driver realized what route he was expected to take, he had considered turning down the fair altogether. Now, with that damnable humming no longer a memory... he vehemently wished that he had. With a sneer, the man glanced back at the compartment. Inside were the two, probably slumbering, passengers whom he couldn't help but blame.

For a series of moments, his thoughts darkened.

Once more, the whip-poor-will sang its shrill, repeating song, sending a shiver through the man's body. He squinted at the coming turn of road. The town of Honning wasn't far. Despite wishing he didn't, the driver still remembered the way. He knew it as well as his own name. With a frown, he cracked the reins–snapping a jolt of urgency into the chestnut mare.

"Do you hear that?"

The young woman peered intently through a window. The sudden lunge of the carriage had caused the book she had been reading to fall into her lap. Missy Allensworth had been on the road for nearly two days, and despite the lateness of the hour, she was currently wide awake. Her fiancé, on the other hand, had been asleep for hours and hardly stirred at the sound of her voice.

"Stewart!" She added some volume.

Stewart Dunn stirred, though his eyes remained closed. "Hmmm? Oh, have we arrived?"

"No, we're still on the road!" The woman's voice was small. "But listen. Do you hear that?"

"It's only a bird, dear. Go back to sleep."

"I wasn't sleeping." Missy straightened her eyeglasses. Brushed a stray bit of hair behind one ear. "And I'm not talking about the whip-poor-will. There's something else." She looked beyond the field, to the coming line of trees. "I think it's coming from the woods."

Stewart sat up, blinked dumbly and tried to listen. "You mean the... kind of a humming sound?" He asked, unsure of much, given his level of cognizance. For her part, Missy looked more excited than nervous. She nodded vigorously.

After two sedentary days, here was something of intrigue which hadn't been printed on a page. It was enough to quicken her heart rate and color her cheeks–this unexpected unknown. Her mother had always discouraged this side of her daughter's personality. Insisting that insatiable curiosity was a trait most unbecoming on a lady. Fortunately, Missy had no designs on becoming one of those.

"Well," Stewart slid down the bench. "What do you think it is?"

Moving his own curtain to one side, he peered out over an expanse of wild grass peppered with small white flowers. These shone like fireflies in the light of the full moon. Beyond the field was the edge of a thick forest which stretched all the way to the distant peaks of mount Washington.

Stewart yawned. "Sounds like machinery. A grist mill, maybe?" With that, he flopped back down onto his bench. "Or crickets?"

Missy stared intently at the distant hum and considered this.

"Probably." Was all she said.

"Ah. Mystery solved, then." Stewart stretched and adjusted the balled up jacket he'd been using for a pillow. "Have to say, a bed would be a nice change of pace."

Missy was inclined to agree, but her fiancé was asleep again before she had a chance to do so. With a sigh, she turned to look once more out the window. The moon was nearly full. She had never been to Massachusetts before and so far, the place was lovely. Strange how the driver had been so adamant on taking the long road from Albany. But following the Hudson all the way to upstate New York would have added an entire extra day to their already lengthy journey and Stewart would hear none of it. Missy knew the trip had him on edge. As much as she wasn't looking forward to going home, her fiancé was going to be meeting her parents for the first time.

This year away had been somewhat harder than she wanted to admit. And while every letter from her mother had been signed with the love of both parents, she couldn't help but wonder what sort of reception was waiting for her back in New Haven. Especially with the skinny Blake-obsessed would-be novelist who had managed to capture her heart. She sighed deeply. Then resolved to concentrate on the mystery out her window. The humming was growing less distant as they went and was most definitely not crickets. Another hour passed before the coach rolled to a stop.

According to the sign, the town was called Honning. Population one hundred and nineteen. It had appeared quite without warning in the middle of the woods. Stewart had slept the entire rest of the way, but not Missy. For her, the closer they came to the treeline, the less sleepy she felt. Though faint here in the town itself, that strange hum had reached its crescendo about a mile back.

She gave a start as the carriage door swung open. Bathed in a stark lantern glow, the driver looked sinister--even disturbed. Missy couldn't help but pull away.

"We'll stay here tonight and get back on the road first thing in the morning. Help you with the bags?"

"Oh." Missy felt bombarded. It was the most she had heard the man say since Albany. "Yes. Thank you."

With a nod, the driver stepped up to unlatch the luggage from where he'd secured on the roof. After shoving her copy of Darwin's 'The Various Contrivances by Which Orchids are Fertilized by Insects' into her hand bag, Missy tapped her fiancé. For his part, Stewart sat up mid-snore looking very confused.

"We're here." She said.

"Oh! Good." Stewart yawned again. "Very good. Driver, where is the nearest..."

"Hotel?" Whispered Missy, hoping the driver hadn't heard the question. "Apparently we're here. Looks charming, actually."

"As long as they have beds..." Stewart said this musically as he stepped down. Before him was a small flight of stairs with ornate wooden railings on either side. This led to the door of a two-story cottage that looked straight out of some lost Brothers Grimm tale. Above the door was a beautifully carved sign.

"Gjestehus?" Stewart read the word as he stepped onto the earthen street. With another yawn, he turned, offering a hand for his fiancé. "Am I delirious, or is that sign written in German?"

"Those options are hardly mutually exclusive, dear." Missy threw both arms around the love of her life, and squeezed for longer than she had intended.

"Darling?" Asked Stewart with a note of surprise. "Are you alright?"

"Yes." She forced a smile. "Just happy to be out of that... carriage." She had wanted to say noise. With a shiver, Missy cast a glare back to the road and the dark forest which swallowed it whole. "Come on. Let's get you to bed."

The next morning came quickly. Stewart Dunn awoke alone in a bed he did not recognize, wearing pajamas he could not recall putting on. If not for the alluring smells of panfried meats, he might never have found the will to get up and lumber downstairs.

Missy was sitting at a long table and appeared lost in thought. Placed before her was a yellow plate supporting a thickly buttered slice of bread and a boiled egg which had been sliced down the middle.

"Morning." Stewart said with a yawn.

"Oh!" Missy snapped back into the moment. Stammered, "Yes. Good morning, dear!" She smiled, offering a cheek, which Stewart kissed.

"How long have you been awake?"

"A while. Brain kept going all night, I'm afraid."

"Oh," Suddenly feeling guilty for getting so much quality sleep, Stewart placed his hand over Missy's. "Are you... nervous about seeing your parents?"

"What? No," Missy sounded surprised. "Well perhaps... but that isn't what I–"

"Coffee, ja?" A large, ruddy-faced woman appeared. Stewart was so startled, he practically jumped.

"Please." Said Missy with a gracious bob of her head. Shortly thereafter, a second plate clanged down. It was the twin of Missy's except that it contained an extra piece of the thick bread. Suddenly aware of his hunger, Stewart lowered himself onto the bench next to his fiancé. The bread was dense and dark, but the butter was the most delicious thing he had ever tasted. Nearly as sweet as honey.

As he chewed, two cups of coffee appeared–both filled with steaming dark liquid. The ruddy-faced woman then set down a small crock of milk.

"Thank you!" Stewart spit crumbs as he spoke. With a snicker, Missy lifted a napkin and dabbed the corners of his mouth.

After flashing a sheepish grin, Stewart looked around the kitchen. There were shelves supporting stacks of yellow plates, crocks, mugs and other dinnerware. The table was old but featured a hand painted trim around the perimeter–a repeating motif of small white flowers and plump honey bees flying between them. After adding a liberal amount of milk to his cup, he offered Missy the same.

Stewart Dunn had been in small town inns before, but the Gjestehus was unique. In many ways, it felt out of place. Almost as if they had awoken in some old fairytale. Fortunately all three rooms had been vacant the night prior. There had been two for the future Mr. and Mrs. Dunn and one for the driver–a surly man, as far as Stewart was concerned. As of yet, he was nowhere to be seen, though it was barely seven o'clock.

"Darling?" Stewart inched a bit closer to his beloved. Touched her hand. "Melissa?"

"Hmm?"

"What's on your mind?"

"Oh..." Missy sighed, offering a weakish sort of smile. "It's my dissertation."

"Your dissertation?"

"Yes."

"You mean, the same dissertation you weren't planning to start for another three years?"

"Yes."

"Ah."

"Don't you 'Ah' me, Stewart Dunn. I know you think my mind is only ever on books and studies, but for a modern woman to succeed in this world of men, she has to be sharp. Sharper by far than the fool I'm taking home for Thanksgiving dinner, anyway."

"Well, that shouldn't be hard." Stewart speared the orange egg yolk with his fork. "Have you decided on a topic?"

At this, Melissa Allensworth turned pale. She lowered her mug and looked around the kitchen. Once certain they were alone, she spoke softly.

"Darling?"

"Yes?" Stewart said, munching on a bit of egg.

"Do you remember the sound we heard last night?"

The two locked eyes. Then Stewart swallowed hard and offered the only detail he could recover from the hazy night prior.

"You mean the crickets?"

"It wasn't crickets." Missy tapped her chin. "Nor was it machinery, or the wind, or my overactive imagination. I'm positive that sound was the droning of hornets or bees. If I were judging on volume alone, I'd say we must have passed an enormous hive. One surely big enough to dwarf even the largest on record." Her voice shrunk inward. "Only... that's impossible."

"Impossible? Why?"

"Because we heard the sound last *night,* darling. And according to every book I've read on the subject... Wasps, hornets and bees are only active during the day." Missy took a small sip of her coffee. "Unless..."

"Unless what?"

"Unless we are dealing with a new species. Something unknown and endemic only to this region. It's very interesting."

Stewart looked as if he were piecing together a puzzle. "If that were true... it would be a wonderful topic for a dissertation."

"Maybe a whole book." Missy's eyes were wide. Her face, bright with possibility. "Of course we'd have to find them first."

The sound of boots on the floor was startling. Missy and Stewart turned at once to see the ragged form of their driver enter the room. He looked as if he had slept even less than she had. He was tall, with a pale beard and a wild look in his eye.

"Good morning," Stewart offered the greeting with half a heart. It was not reciprocated. The driver sat on the opposite end of the table–facing forward, saying nothing. Less than a minute later, the large serving woman appeared again with a plate of bread, egg and a curved length of sausage. Without a word of thanks, the man began to consume what he had been given in large, hurried bites.

"I want to be moving in half an hour." Said the driver between chews. "Just need to see to the horse and we'll be off."

Stewart nodded. "Wonderful. Thank you."

The man grunted. Then he gulped down the rest of his food and stood up. On his way out of the kitchen, he nearly barreled into a tall bus boy who was coming in. No more than twenty, the boy wore a stained shirt, an apron and a look of surprise. His complexion was pale, but the bone structure was the same as the large woman who had served them already. He picked up the driver's plate and untouched cup of coffee, then shuffled out the way he came.

"I should have liked some sausage." Stewart grumbled into his still steaming cup.

"Darling?" Missy's voice had that half-sweet-half-vinegar quality she used whenever her mind was already made up. "I think you should tell our driver that we shall be staying part of the day."

Stewart choked on a mouthful of hot liquid.

"Yes," Missy nodded, agreeing with her own idea. "I definitely think you should do that. I know he's is in a hurry, but we've been on the road for two days already. Surely a break of a few more hours won't be too much to ask. Tell him we'll leave later this afternoon."

"But..." Stewart scrambled for purchase on his current mental ledge. "What about your parents? You sent them a telegram back in Albany. If we're late to arrive, won't they worry?"

Appearing unmoved, Missy dabbed her mouth with a corner of embroidered napkin.

"Probably."

Stewart simply did now know what to say. So far, he had managed to keep a lid on his bundled anxieties, but this sudden change of plans was simply too much for barely seven in the morning. His stomach was already tied into knots at the prospect of meeting his fiancé's well-to-do family for the first time. Especially after he had demonstrated enough gall to propose to their daughter, without as much as writing for their permission.

Though asking for Missy's hand had felt like the most correct thing he had ever done, Stewart knew that it had caused an equal and opposite reaction. His very own personal sword of Damocles, was waiting for him in Connecticut, and it was poised to fall upon his very own personal neck. The thought had plagued him for months. Allowing anticipation and dread to build steadily inside like steam in a teapot.

And now they were going to be late.

Almost cheerfully, Missy swung both legs over the bench and stood up. "I'm going to get changed into something more appropriate."

"More appropriate for what?"

"Just some light field work, darling. Nothing to worry about." Missy planted a gentle kiss on the young man's face. "I was very particular last night in noting where we were when the insect song was loudest. Can't be more than a mile northeast of here. Somewhere in the woods, I should think."

"You want us to hike into the woods? Today?"

"Oh yes, definitely. And as soon as possible." Seeing it was needed, she placed a hand on her fiancé's cheek. "This is important, and not just for the dissertation. It's a hive, Stewart. I know it is. One big enough for the sound to carry almost a mile. What sort of entomologist would I be if every cell in my body wasn't aching to know what made such a thing?"

Stewart sighed, but offered no argument.

"All I need is to see it for myself. To get some field notes, a location–maybe a sketch or two. Then we get right back on the road to New Haven. I promise! Another time we can come back with more supplies and document it the right way. I know you want me to leave it alone, but..."

"No," Stewart said. "I don't want you to do that."

As the two embraced, both believed they were alone in the quaint, eat-in kitchen of the Gjestehus. But from the nook of an unseen pantry, the tall bus boy stood in silence. Right then he was biting at a hangnail... trying to decide what on earth he was going to do.

Less than an hour later, the future Mr. and Mrs. Dunn stood in the brisk autumn air. The main road in Honning stretched between a dense woodland. Despite being the middle of November, snow had yet to fall in the Western part of the state. But this fact did not deny the wind its teeth. Stewart winced, turning away from the sudden gust.

Missy lifted the collar of her slate blue jacket with a gloved hand.

"In the forest, the trees should shield us." She said this somewhat distantly–double checking the pockets of her coat. Through the thick wool, her hands detected a small notepad, two pencils, a tin specimen box and something hard and round–roughly the size of a pocket watch. This last item, she retrieved and held out flat in her palm. The compass' needle spun wildly at first, eventually deciding which way was north.

"Darling," Stewart fastened the final button of his jacket collar. "Let's be quick about this, shall we? This whole place feels off. Like it was transplanted from the foot of the Swiss Alps or something."

"We are Swedish here," said a small, unexpected voice. "From a little village on the island of Öland."

Standing in the street, looking quite nervous was the Gjestehus' server boy. In the sun, his disheveled hair was very blonde.

"I overheard you at breakfast, Miss. About what you heard last night on the road." The boy threw cautionary glances up and down the street. "Everyone in Honning has heard that sound. Most won't say the name aloud anymore but... we call it the *Grendel hive.*"

Missy gasped. "So it *is* a hive."

The boy looked around like he didn't want to be seen. After absently kicking a rock, he spoke again.

"Why do you want to find it?"

"Oh. Well," Missy thought for a few seconds before saying more. "Insects *fascinate* me. They always have. I read about them, study them. I would very much like to write about them too, though I will need something to say. Something new." She pursed her lips into a smile. "I suspect that, somewhere in these woods, you have a species belonging to the order hymenoptera which diverges significantly from any on record. The night activity alone was enough to pique my interest but after everything you just said." For a moment, Missy fell inward–into a dozen possibilities that she wisely decided not to go into. "Yes. I would like to find this Grendel hive of yours very much."

"Okay," Somehow, the boy gave a look that was equal parts relieved and nervous. "Then we'd better get going. Bad things happen in the woods at night."

Missy found apprehension on Stewart's face, but gave a quick nod.

"Yes, well--as it happens we were hoping to finish this up before lunch," She smiled. "What's your name, boy?"

"Oscar," said the boy. "But you won't need that compass. I know the way."

For a quarter of an hour, the tall boy led the couple through the woods. He'd been following an old footpath that alternated between difficult and nigh-impossible to see.

"The founders of Honning were beekeepers. Mead makers." Oscar said this unprompted after a long silence. "Once, Honning had many hives." The boy looked to the ground. Bit his lip. "They are all gone now. Destroyed. It happened when I was very small." Reluctantly, the boy turned to stare into the woods. "The bees inside were torn apart. Wings and heads, legs and little bodies, all dead and covered in something sticky and black. Something like honey."

"Wow." Though he had been teetering between frustration and boredom, Stewart's ears perked up. "Black honey? Bees torn apart inside their hives?" Realizing he was sounding a bit too excited, Stewart cleared his throat, calmed his expression. "I mean... that's awful."

"Yes." Said the boy. "Very awful. For a town full of mead makers, the bees were our whole life."

"Ah. How true." Stewart pressed on more gently, though his fiction writer's imagination was ablaze. "So what happened? What sort of thing can tear thousands of little insects limb from limb? Are you saying it was the hive we heard last night?"

"That sound... it is a shadow that hangs over our town." The boy looked ready to explode into either violence or tears, "And like a shadow, we cannot grasp it."

Suddenly, it donned on Missy that Oscar was wearing neither hat, nor coat. To her, he suddenly looked very cold, but that might have been a trick of his fair complexion.

"That is terrible of course but, not completely unheard of," Missy's thought drifted inward. "Certain wasps have been known to do this. Sometimes they will wipe out an entire population but... I've never heard of it happening in domesticated hives before."

The boy had no response for this.

Minutes passed with only the sounds of crunching leaves to accompany Missy's thoughts. Her mind was busy scanning long-ago read pages. Books containing passages on the complexities of insect societies and behavior. Nothing about what Oscar was describing seemed right, but that didn't mean it wasn't possible. Plenty of unlikely things were scoffed at by science before being properly documented and published. The platypus being a famous example.

Perhaps this really was her chance. Her moment to shine. Attempting to hide the resulting surge of excitement, Missy bit her lip. Following the tall server boy, she stepped around a tree and turned south. Just ahead and off to the side there was a line of visible path that led to an oddly toppled pine. Odd because it was suspended in mid-air–supported by a pair of still healthy trees which had no choice but to bear the weight of their fallen sibling.

As he kneeled down, Oscar placed one hand upon the cold, leaf-laden earth and looked at the base of the fallen tree. It looked hollow–rotten from within. The surface of the wood was black as tar, as was the dirt around it. For a series of long uncomfortable moments, Missy and Stewart both had the idea that the boy was praying. Perhaps to some axe-wielding pagan god with braids in his beard.

"Oscar?" Missy approached the kneeling boy, touching his shoulder.

"I'm sorry," Oscar's voice was grim. His eyes focused on the blackened earth. "It's just... I haven't been here in a long time. This is where they found her. My sister."

Missy gasped at the implication. She withdrew her hand and allowed the following silence to grow.

"Olivia had just turned six." Oscar said at last. "She was wearing the scarf mormor had knitted for her birthday. No one would let me see her so I snuck into the mortician's basement." As the boy spoke, his words grew cold. "Her arms, legs and face were covered in welts. Big ones–hard and black. Some the size of teacups. They tried to wipe her clean, but I saw them. The dark stains on her skin. Her face."

"Black honey." Stewart whispered the words without meaning to.

Oscar sniffed, then he gave a nod. "She was too little. She didn't understand what stalks these woods at night... and neither do you."

A lick of wind slipped through the trees, turning Missy's head. When she opened her eyes, they beheld the path behind. The one that led back to a strange little village and a coach which was waiting so impatiently to take her home. Thinking about it all, she couldn't help but shudder.

"Oscar... I'm so sorry. I..." Missy struggled to find the right words. "I didn't know bees could do that."

The boy stood up. Brushed some dirt off his legs. "I never said they were bees." The statement hung in the air before the boy resumed his slow but determined lead. "Look, all I know is that every night I lie awake, listening. Whatever those buzzing things really are, their song laughs at my grief. Tells me to give up. To let them take me... just like they took my sister."

The circles under the boy's eyes seemed darker than before. From a pocket, he produced a small bottle which Missy recognized as lamp oil.

"The only way to lift Honning's curse is to find the Grendel hive during the day. When they sleep."

"My God," Missy sounded shocked but also crestfallen as her plans of a career-launching dissertation turned abruptly to ash. "You're going to burn it, aren't you?"

Oscar's smile was a chilling thing. "I'm sure as hell going to try."

Finally, after nearly forty minutes trudging through thick woodland, the path spilled into a clearing. Missy blinked at the change in light, focusing on what looked like the remains of an old homestead. The unlikely spot was overgrown and untended--abandoned by all who ever had ever known it was there. In the center of what looked to be a half acre, stood the foundation and blackened skeleton of a house. Right away, Missy could see old timbers, a door frame, part of a wall. The evidence of a horrendous blaze extended to the toppled remains of six stilted structures. Hives, she knew. All broken and burned.

"Those were bee boxes." She said for Stewart's benefit, albeit with a note of tragedy in her voice. "Looks like the Langstroth design."

"I can't believe you can even tell." He replied, approaching where the main house had stood. "If I'm being honest, this place gives me the creeps. Reminds me of the witch's house from that Brother's Grimm story. The one with the two German kids and the bread crumbs."

"They've *all* got German kids," Missy teased. "Hansel and Grendel?"

"That's the one." Stewart snapped his fingers.

As he surveying more of the house' remains, the humor drained from the writer's face. When he spoke again it was in a whisper only his fiancé could hear.

"But this isn't some fairytale. This place was a home. A life. And now it's just sitting here, waiting to be forgotten." Leaning over, he peered down into an earthen cellar filled with various blackened debris. Boards, smashed barrels, part of a table. "It's incredibly tragic... but also fascinating, you know?"

Missy put a hand on the man's back. "Still wishing we were sitting in that coach right now?"

"Technically, yes," Stewart kissed her hand. "But now that we're here, I'm all for pressing on. Maybe we'll both end up with something worth writing about."

Feeling a swell of warmth, Missy squeezed her would-be novelist, then looked for their guide.

"Oscar," She spoke up as the boy was some distance away. "Whose house was this?"

The boy turned, looking somewhat overwhelmed. "It... it belonged to the Grendels. Burgess and Esmé founded Honning with the rest of my people, but... they preferred to keep to themselves."

"Oh?" Missy began walking. "What happened to them?"

"No one knows. But they disappeared around the same time as the attacks on our hives began to happen. I know that someone from town was sent to warn them of what had happened... but Burgess and Esmé were already gone."

"What about the hives?" The question was Stewart's. "Destroyed like the all rest?"

"Actually, no." admitted Oscar, "The boxes were found toppled and broken but, empty. No torn apart little bodies, no black honey. The bees were just gone. But... they didn't stay that way. As I said, I was little at the time, but I've heard the stories my whole life. The buzzing would come at night--always at night. And in the morning, the remains of another family's hives would be found. Eventually, people came to blame the Grendels, since, in their eyes the trouble started here."

The boy knelt down to pick up a blackened acorn. After turning it over in his hands, he tossed it at the house.

"If..." Stewart sounded very serious. "The things that live in this Grendel hive aren't bees... what *are* they?"

"You have to understand," said the boy. "Sweden is an ancient place. And when my people came here, I fear they brought more from the old country than they meant to." Oscar's tone was flat, distant and resigned. "The stories call them draugr."

"Drowger?" Missy said the word, failing to match the boy's pronunciation.

"It is an old viking word." The boy stepped over a blackened timber. "Mormor described them as things of the earth. Spirits that have grown restless after being dead for too long. She said the draugr will sometimes come up from the cold ground–out of the dark places where light cannot reach. They have the power to possess the living. But for that to happen... mormor said that the draugr must first be... *kalla på*. I think the word is, *summoned*."

"Of course," Missy did not sound quite as enthralled as her fiancé. "Evil spirits came out of the ground and whisked away the Grendels before systematically wiping out every bee in Honning. Then, rather than search for a rational explanation, the good people of your village decided to march here and burn the entire place to the ground. Am I getting all this right?"

Sensing the woman's hostility, Oscar turned to meander a bit farther down the length of the farm. When there was enough distance between them and the boy, Stewart turned with a look of concern.

"Darling?"

"Yes?"

"What was *that* for?"

Missy shrugged. "These... *people*. They have encountered a species of insect currently unknown to science and their first impulse is to label it as *evil* and burn it off the face of the earth. Lots of organisms prey on other organisms, it doesn't make them devil-possessed."

"I think you mean *draugr*-possessed." Stewart alone snickered at this. "Darling, listen." He was speaking in that same private whisper again. "I know you're concerned about the scientific implications of this discovery but, even if you can overlook all the strangeness, or the fact that these people had their livelihoods literally ripped apart... *something killed that boy's sister.*"

Missy sighed, "I *know*." She said this with too much ire for her own liking. "I know."

By the time she looked over, the boy had shuffled over to a ramshackle tool shed in the south-eastern quadrant of the farm. Inexplicably, it was the only structure which had not been burned. After cooling down for a bit, the woman began to feel guilty for snapping at the boy. After all, he'd only been the messenger.

"Come on," Stewart gently touched the small of her back. "Let's have a look."

After expelling a quick breath, Missy nodded and the pair made their way over to the shed. Inside, Oscar was already looking over the contents. Missy could see rusty shovels, garden tools, sealed jars, some old rabbit traps and the leaves from who knew how many autumns, strewn over it all.

"So... why wasn't this burned this too?" She asked as kindly as possible.

"I don't know that either." The boy sounded defensive. Absently, he brushed a few leaves from the surface of one shelf, revealing a large pair of shears. These he picked up to inspect. The metal was covered in flakes of reddish rust, and in some spots, had oxidized to a deep green.

"Iron." Oscar said with a note of reverence.

Missy nodded. "Is that... *helpful* somehow?"

"Well, maybe. Mormor used to say," He looked at the woman then turned away. "Never mind."

"No. Please," Missy touched the boy's arm. "Please go on."

"Well," the boy shrugged. "She sometimes talked about the old weapons. Things like fire and other things. She said one way to banish the draugr from a body was by placing a pair of iron sheers upon the chest. But... I guess that sounds really stupid."

Though she very much thought that it did, in fact, sound stupid, Missy did not want to insult the boy or his culture a second time. She just wanted to understand. "No it doesn't," She winked. "You should bring them. Just in case."

Oscar snapped the sheers closed and slipped them into his belt so the handle stuck out like the hilt of a sword. After that, he smiled.

"Well, look at that." Missy's eyes were set upon a mason jar--one of many that had been sealed and stocked over a decade prior. It was filled with rounded green leaves. "Do you know what these are?"

The boy shook his head.

"Broadleaf plantain." With some effort, she twisted off the lid. "A common plant used by apiarists and gardeners for treating a variety of rashes... and bee stings. You take a leaf, chew it into a pulp and apply to the injection site. Then you just wrap it up tight and you're done! It draws out the venom--works wonders." Gently, the woman smiled. Then, after removing three leaves from the jar, she slipped them into a pocket.

"I believe in science, Oscar. What I can learn from a book. The rest, I admit, is hard for me."

Missy looked up at the boy for a second or two, just wanting to say more.

"Um... hello?" Stewart's voice called from outside. It sounded a short distance away. "I've found something you both might want to have a look at."

Stewart's hand was on his head--punctuating a full body expression of disbelief.

Before him was an old blackened husk of what had once been a tree. The trunk had neither branches nor crown but terminated in a yawning opening roughly six feet from the base. It looked almost as if the tree's upper half had been broken off and discarded. Most notable was the charcoal hue which was darkest by the roots. Seeing it reminded Stewart of the toppled pine they'd passed earlier. The place where the boy's sister had been found. Thinking of it sent a chill up his spine.

He reached out and touched the wood–tracing one of the many strange symbols that had been carved there. The characters were part letter, part picture and utterly foreign. Instinctively, he cupped both hands around one ear and placed them on the surface. Then he closed his eyes and just listened. So intent was he in the task, Stewart didn't notice how the ground was reacting to his presence. How his weight was, ever so slightly, causing the area around him to sink.

"Darling?" Missy's voice jarred Stewart back into his shoes. "What did you find?"

"Well," Stewart straightened, clapping his hands off the sides of his pants. "To be blunt... your sound."

"What?" Missy began walking faster. "Right there?! *Inside the tree*?!"

"That's not possible," Oscar sounded defensive. "My... my people clearly checked there. Look. It's been burned!"

"Actually, I don't think it was," Stewart brushed the trunk lightly with his fingers. Tracing something like a letter X but with antlers. "The wood may be black but I don't think the damage is from fire. There's some kind of tacky residue here." He sniffed the tips of his thumb and forefinger. "It smells... *sweet*."

The phrase 'black honey' ran through Missy's mind, though she refused to say it aloud.

Half running, the boy crossed the distance and pressed his face against the tree."

"He's right!" Oscar sounded elated. "I can hear it! That sound... I can't believe it. The hive was right here all the time." The boy pulled away from the tree with a look of dark triumph. "The draugr," he said. "They must have been using this thing like a tunnel."

"Or a chimney," Nodded Stewart with widening eyes. "Their own personal way in and out of hell."

Just then, the final stanza of a poem drifted through the mind of the would-be novelist. Despite everything that was going on, he began to recite a little Blake. "Into my garden stole... when the night had veiled the pole. In the morning glad I see... my foe outstretched beneath the tree."

When he looked at Missy there was fear in her eyes. More alarming than that, the woman was backing away.

"Stewart, the ground! The ground is..."

But Stewart never heard what the ground was.

Before Missy's statement could be completed, the man, the boy, the rotten old tree and close to ten feet of earth, dropped most inexplicably into the ground.

The eyes of Melissa Allensworth opened slowly and with effort.

Muffled shouts were coming from nearby. Possibly they were under water. And indeed, when she reached up to touch the throbbing place on the back of her head, her fingers came back wet. For a moment or two, she was unable to comprehend the blood which glistened there.

"Melissa!"

She heard her name more clearly.

"Missy darling, are you alright?"

Energy flooded back into her limbs. She sat up, then looked down at the large rock which was currently painted the same color as her fingers.

"Melissa, answer me, please!"

The shouts were no longer underwater.

"I'm here!" She shouted back. "I'm okay."

"Oh thank God!" Stewart sounded like he was crying.

Missy got to her feet and fought through the sudden counter rush of pain which filled her skull. Where the tree and two people had stood only moments ago was now a great, gaping hole. Approaching in utter disbelief, she saw it was deep–maybe a story and a half. In it were the smashed remains of the tree, a boy who looked to be favoring one arm and Stewart Dunn.

"Thank God, you're alright, darling." Said the man in the ground. "We've been shouting for hours."

"What?" Missy almost fell back again. "*Hours*?!"

"Well it feels like hours," Stewart said. "Hard to tell. I lost my watch."

Right then Missy looked up to see the sky had indeed changed.

"Just hold on." She shouted, running. "I'll find something to get you out of there."

Upon reaching the tool shed, Missy looked around frantically.

"Is there a ladder, or maybe some rope?" Stewart's voice sounded so far away.

"No, nothing like that!" Panic was rising in the woman's chest. "But there's a shovel! Maybe I could dig you out?"

"That'll take too long." Now Oscar was doing the shouting. He sounded like he was in a lot of pain. "Remember, we don't have long. When the sun goes down, the draugr will come."

"He's right," said Stewart. "Oh God, I can hear them. There's a tunnel over there, but I don't want to know where it leads. Please Missy, get back to town. Get help and hurry back."

"No, Stewart... I can't leave you."

"As long as you come back," He said. "You won't be leaving anyone."

Missy was suddenly furious. She hated being told what she couldn't do almost as much as she hated feeling powerless. "Fine," She said. "Here." She tossed the shovel down into the far side of the pit. "See what you can do with that. Maybe it'll take less time to dig than you think."

"I'll certainly try. Just please be quick. I love you."

I love you too. That's what Missy wanted to say, but her legs were already moving as fast as they could. She sped out of the Grendel farm and back into the woods. The path they had followed was easy to spot at first, but that changed. There were too many turns, too many forks that she didn't recall. And every time she had to retrace and rethink, the sky aged just a little more.

By the time Missy finally shot out of the woods and back onto the main street of Honning, it was nearly dusk. Out of breath, out of time, she didn't know where to turn.

"Well, well," The voice sounded gruff and none too pleased. "Look who finally showed up."

She turned to see the hard face of the man whom she had hired back in Albany. The driver was walking toward a coach that had been ready and hitched all day.

"Where in the hell have you been?"

Missy rushed to the man and tried to answer, but her words cracked and broke upon his chest. Reaching under the driver's seat, the man retrieved a canteen and handed it over. Unscrewing the cap, the woman drank greedily in a series of deep gulps.

"Please," Her eyes were wild. Bulging and rimmed with pink like a panicked horse. "I need... Stewart is... *they are coming*! The... the *drowger*!" she turned back and listened for a second. Praying. Dreading. "The damned Grendel woman's bees!"

The name brought a visible change in the man. The frustration he had been holding onto all day simply melted away. In its place was a grave expression. One that was ready to believe every word this half-crazed woman might say.

"Alright, just calm down and breathe. Tell me everything."

After another pull from the canteen, Missy did exactly that. She told the man about the sound she'd first heard on the road and how she had stayed up all night thinking about what it might mean, both to science and her career. She described the tall bus boy who had become their guide and the terrible things he'd shared on the way to the Grendel farm. When her account reached the tree, and where she's left her companions, Missy's voice hitched. Finishing was hard, but she pushed through.

"And then..." She let out a shuddering breath. "That's when I saw you."

Missy looked up, expecting to be either dismissed or, possibly, committed. Instead, the driver calmly placed a hand upon her shoulder. Then, he turned to another man who was passing by.

"You there!" The driver said more than this, but the rest was in Swedish. When through, he held up two fingers and repeated one of the words. "Två! Understand?"

The other man nodded and ran off.

Wasting no time, the driver dove back under the seat where the canteen had been. This time, the search produced a tangled bundle of rope and a large wooden mallet.

"Tell me. How deep was this hole in the ground?" His words were short and full of urgency.

"Oh," Missy's mind raced. "A story or more. Maybe twenty feet?"

Hearing this, the man took down two lanterns hanging from hooks on the coach. The second, he pushed towards the woman.

"One for each of us. Okay?"

Missy accepted the lantern and swallowed hard.

"Okay. Thank you," she said... "I'm sorry, I don't remember your name."

"Probably because you never asked for it." Grumbled the man as he slipped the mallet through a belt loop in his pants. "Just call me Anders." He said this with no gravity whatsoever and left no room for reply. The passerby had returned. He was rushing forth with two wooden stakes.

"Två." He said proudly.

After this, the men exchanged another couple sentences in Swedish before the passerby looked directly at Missy.

"The sun is nearly down, Miss. You'll never make it."

"We have to." Was all she said.

The flight back to the Grendel farm was a frantic dash--aided by a path only Anders could see. When they arrived, the sun was much too low for comfort.

"They were right there!" At the edge of the hole, Missy shook her head in exasperation. "Maybe they dug themselves out?"

Unconvinced, Anders knelt down. "Don't think so." He extended a thick finger indicating the ragged edges of earth. "The only signs of digging are down there. Looks like they didn't get very far."

Missy could see the shovel. It was down in the dark, laying just beside some newly moved soil.

Anders shook out the bundle of rope until it resembled what it really was, a ladder. One end was placed roughly five feet from the hole. Then, with the help of the mallet, both stakes were banged into the ground. Once secure, the ladder's other end was tossed in the hole.

"From my sailing days." The look on Ander's face was hard and serious. "Never know when you're going to need it. Come on."

In silence the two strangers descended. Stepping on the wooden rungs of the ladder, taking care not to drop their respective lanterns. Down in the earth, the humming sound was undeniable. It crept under Missy's skin, finding the softest places of her throat and stomach. When Anders held out a match, the woman swung her lantern close enough for it to flicker to life.

The ground was a mess. Akin to freshly tilled topsoil, it was soft, loose and difficult to walk on. There were footprints around. But footprints only.

"It doesn't make sense." The panic in her voice was impossible to control as she rounded what was left of the tree. "Where could they have gone?"

"This must have taken you a long time to hollow out. Didn't it, Bayla?"

Missy felt confused but said nothing. Her eyes darted hungrily as she pushed the lantern's glow from one shadow to the next. Eventually, something gleamed. The iron sheers were buried but for a small curve of handle. Missy picked them up, tapped off the soil and turned them over in her hand.

"What's that?" The voice of Anders caught her by surprise.

"Maybe nothing." Missy didn't believe iron had any magical providence over the forces of evil, but she couldn't deny that in her hand, the object felt like a weapon. She slid the sheers into her belt the way Oscar had done.

The driver had already moved around the tree. He was standing at the far end of the chamber, holding his lantern high. Beyond him, Missy could see the yawning pitch dark mouth of a passage.

"That's right." She gasped. "Stewart did say something about a tunnel. Maybe they tried to find another way out?"

"If your friends went down there, Miss... I don't think it was by choice. Look at the ground."

Trembling, Missy forced the lantern's glow upon the ground. Marks led down into the dark of the tunnel. Not footprints but a pair of wide grooves--as if two heavy somethings had been dragged.

Missy gasped, then crossed her chest. "Oh Stewart. My darling. This is all my fault."

Anders frowned, "Not so, Miss." He grumbled. "Had I not been such a damned coward, I could have ended this years ago."

As the two trudged on, the mind of Melissa Allensworth scrambled for purchase.

She'd always known that field work came with its dangers, but this was something else. Worse still--the absence of her fiancé was causing her physical pain. Missy had to find him. But to do that, she was going to have to silence the rational half of her brain--the one still convinced that nothing she was experiencing was possible outside the realm of fiction.

"Who's Bayla?" Missy's voice was a tiny, trembling thing.

Anders jumped at the sudden voice, but said nothing.

"You just said that name," Asserted Missy, "So who is Bayla? I thought the Grendel woman's name was Esmé."

"That's true." The man frowned, then released a long breath through his nose. "Esmé Elisabeth Callander in her youth. She was a gift from God. Beautiful, endlessly caring and a truly gifted beekeeper. But... Esmé had another side. Almost as if there was an entire other person living inside her. It was so strange the first time I saw it happen. The change was quick--a second, maybe two. It would wash over her face and eyes, as one went away and the other took over."

"Bayla." Missy shuddered. "Bayla was the other."

Anders nodded. "And where Esmé was kind, Bayla was jealous, paranoid, even cruel. You see, *that* was the reason the Grendels chose to live separate from Honning. Burgess didn't want anyone to think his wife was mad or worse, possessed."

"*Possessed*?"

"Remember where we are, Miss. This is Massachusetts. A place where women were once burned at the stake for growing the wrong kind of weeds in their garden." Anders sighed in frustration. "For her part, Esmé accepted the seclusion, but Bayla grew to despise Burgess. She said he was ashamed of his wife. That all he really wanted was spend more time with a pretty blonde seamstress in town. Strange... I do not recall her name." The man's tone was nostalgic.

"It sounds like you knew her well. Esmé Grendel."

The man averted his eyes. "Better than most. Yes. You see, Burgess was my brother. And my unforgivable sin--that for which I will *burn for all eternity in the fires of hell...* is that I loved my brother's wife."

"Oh." The woman said this with sudden understanding. After a few seconds, she asked something that sounded to her like more of a Stewart question.

"What about Esmé? Who did she love?"

The man looked up with tears in the corners of his pale, lamplit eyes. His mouth opened, then closed as fear flickered across his face.

"We have arrived."

Missy looked ahead to see that they had reached the end of the tunnel. Beyond was a space steeped in darkness. A space that hummed so loudly, she could barely form thoughts.

"Listen to me now." Anders' face was no comfort in the dancing firelight. "Whatever we find in there, your only concern must be your husband. Don't concern yourself with the boy from the Gjestehus and especially don't worry about me. Just find your husband and go. Can you do that?"

"I... I think so."

"*Promise* me."

But Missy didn't want to promise. She *wanted* to protest. Wanted to remind Anders that Stewart wasn't her husband--not yet. Because the two weren't technically going to be married until the spring since that was when the Mayflowers would be in bloom. Instead, with a slew of rising emotions, she gave a reluctant nod.

"Good." Anders placed a large hand on the woman's shoulder. "Just get him back to the ladder. If he can't climb, get underneath him. Stack him on top of you and let your shoulders bear the weight. And forget the lantern, you'll need both hands to do the climbing. It won't be easy but I promise you can do it. Okay?"

"Okay." Missy swallowed. Nodded. Then, after wiping a tear from her cheek, she touched the handle of the rusty iron sheers.

As the two stepped out into the adjoining chamber, neither had the courage to breathe.

The meager light they'd brought caused the perfect shadows to retreat back into the walls. Eventually, two bodies were revealed. She could see a man and a tall boy of around twenty. Neither was moving.

"Stewart!" Missy rushed over and dove to the man's side. "Darling! Wake up. Come on now, it's alright. We just have to go!"

A pulse was located. It was weak but steady. Though she could not rouse him, Missy knew her fiancé was still alive. And for now, that was enough. Using the lantern, she began checking his exposed skin for any wounds or lacerations, almost choking when one was discovered. There was a massive welt on the side of Stewart's neck. Terrible and black–practically the size of a teacup.

"The far wall. There's something... something..." Anders' voice was nearly drowned out by an omnipresent, non-directional droning. Missy looked over to see the large man was standing further into the space–holding his lantern high. Though visibility was poor, she could see the *something* that could only be the Grendel hive.

None of what she was seeing made sense. Missy's mind raced to justify but came up wanting.

Six feet high, more than that across, the structure's surface was composed of black honeycombs. These were stacked in haphazard layers and were leaking a glistening tar that seemed unbound by the forces of gravity. Streams of the stuff were leaking down, but also up to the cavern's ceiling. This simple yet impossible fact caused the woman's rational, scientific mind to fracture. She could feel it–the membrane between sanity and madness was thin in this place.

Suddenly, something shifted–just left of center where the shadows were at their thickest. There was a form protruding from the Grendel hive. Something with arms connected to shoulders, and what might be a head.

Melissa Allensworth should not have been looking. She was supposed to pay attention to her would-be novelist and nothing else. She had agreed that Stewart was all that mattered, and yet, as Anders' light fell upon that collection of body parts sticking out of the honeycomb wall, Missy couldn't help but see what her mind insisted was the upper half of a person.

Her father, for all his flaws, had always told her to trust her own senses above all else. It was why she had insisted they stop to investigate in the first place. Because of what had reached her ears on the road to a remote village in Massachusetts no one had ever heard of.

With renewed vigor, Missy began slapping Stewart's face. But as her own tears streamed, her eyes fell once more to that horrible black carbuncle on his neck. The thing looked as if it were ready to burst. But squeezing the welt only made Stewart convulse before going still again.

It was all too much.

In despair, Missy fell upon the chest of her dearest love, wanting nothing more than to give up. That was when she felt the cold metal of the sheers press into her side. Remembering that just like fire, iron can be a powerful weapon.

The memory of Oscar's words pulled her away from the heaving sobs, and gave her a terrible idea. One that flew in the face of even the most rudimentary knowledge of first aid. She brandished the sheers, forced them open. The metal was old and covered in rust but, by God, it held an edge.

Hand trembling, Missy pressed the metal to the center of the revolting welt. Then she drew her hand away causing what looked like black honey to ooze from the incision.

Oblivious to all of this, the man called Anders had moved to within an arm's length of the central figure. It was stick-skinny and grey in color, but the arms, torso and lower half of a face were undeniably human. Black tar or poison honey, the sticky slime covered the figure's back and most of the skull, leaking down the shoulders in long liquid strands that approximated hair.

"Esmé?" Anders gasped, holding a hand to his mouth.

At the sound of the man's voice, the thing stirred. Hanging arms twitched, fingers curled with the sleepy memory of life before going slack once more. After a few seconds, Anders, swallowed hard, found his nerve to speak again. Just one word.

"Bayla."

Immediately, the wretch took a long draft of stale air. The head perked up and slowly turned to face the man who had spoken its name. There were thin lips, a partially collapsed nose and only one visible eye. It was too large, too bulbous–protruding just slightly from the socket and quivering like jelly with every movement. Upon that oil-black surface, the light from Anders' lantern was reflected in a single orange dot.

The lips flexed. The lower jaw went slack and then began to work as if trying to produce speech. When no sound came, the thing seemed to become frustrated. It leaned forward, straightening a thoroughly bent spine. The sound that rose was the same they had heard before. The very thing that had plagued the village of Honning for these long years. It was the deafening hum of a thousand bees. And this time, it formed a question.

"YOU?"

"Yes! It is Anders!" The man held out placating hands. "What are these horrible things? God in heaven, what have they done to you?"

"MY LOVES..." The insect-song-voice was growing less scattered–clearer somehow. "THEY WERE HERE ALWAYS. BUT BELOW. FORGOTTEN FOR SO LONG. I CALLED FOR YOU FIRST, SWEET ANNNDERSS... BUT YOU WENT AWAY. YOU LEFT ME WITH HIM."

"I had to! My God, don't you see?! Don't you remember? You were his wife, Esmé!"

"I REMEMBER EVERYTHING."

"Then you know what we were doing was a sin! I loved you then, and in fifteen years I have loved no one since. But the two of you were married in God's eyes. I had no choice. I *had* to leave. For all his flaws, Burgess did not deserve–"

"OHHH... BURGESSSS DISSSSERRRVED EVERYTHING." This came in a forceful hiss, that caused dark saliva to fly from the thing's mouth. "ALL AND MORE."

"Oh God." He was openly weeping now. "Oh dear, sweet God."

"GOD? BUT WHICH GOD DO YOU CRY FOR, SWEET ANNDERSS?" The thing aimed its one gelatinous eye upward. "THERE ARE MANY."

That eye was hard to look at. Everything was. Anders had to fight to remain lucid... maybe even sane.

"I REMEMBER CARVING THE RUNES INTO THE SIDE OF A TREE. SPEAKING THE OLD WORDS."

One of the bee-things landed on Anders' ear. He slapped it away, shuddering in a wave of revulsion.

"WHEN MY LOVES FIRST ARRIVED, THEY WERE BUT WHISPERS AND SHADOW. SPIRITS IN NEED OF FORM. SAD SOFT ESMÉ WAS

AFRAID TO INVITE THEM INSIDE... BUT I GAVE THEM WHAT THEY NEEDED AND MORE. NOT JUST ONE BODY... BUT THOUSANDSS."

The infernal buzzing voice was beginning to creep into Anders' brain. The words came from the ceiling and the black combs which lined the walls-- seemingly everywhere but from the thing speaking them. Though its jaw was working lazily, the lips of the Grendel hive were far too receded to form real speech.

"INSIDE MY BEES, MY LOVES DID WHAT YOU REFUSED TO DO, SWEET ANNNDERS. THEY CLAIMED ME WITH PRIDE. HELD ME TIGHT. THEY SAVED ME."

"Is that what you call this? Being *saved*?!" Anders looked around the floor, at the mixture of piled honeycomb and dirt and tar. Then he again met the terrible eye of the thing he had once loved. "What did you do to him?" He asked this flatly. "To my brother?"

With that, the thing's black eye bulged from the socket just a little more-- quivering with what might have been a very old, very well-tended hatred.

"OHHH MY DEAR HUSSSBANND IS HERE. HE IS ALL AROUND AND INSIDE US." The thing gestured to the part of the hive approximately where her stomach would be. "LOOK. SEE THE STUFF OF OUR POISON LOVE. HOW IT FLOWS FROM THIS PLACE. HOW IT SPREADS."

Right then, the object Anders had taken for a bulging black eye, promptly extruded itself and crawled out onto a desiccated cheek. The thing was no insect, only a poor facsimile. A twisted parody with a globular, featureless head that jiggled as it moved. Anders watched in horror as wings like tattered parchment spread and carried the buzzing nightmare away.

"SOON ALL WILL KNOW OUR LOVE."

"Esmé, please..."

"NOT ESSMMÉ!!"

The Grendel Hive shrieked in a voice created not by the vibration of vocal chords, but by the rising hum of a thousand thousand wings. All at once, more and more of the tiny things that were not bees, nor wasps, nor anything natural, poured from the desiccated hag who had once been Esmé Grendel-- swirling like a black whirlwind, filling the room and the gaping mouth of a man called Anders. Instinctively, his jaw snapped shut. Teeth crunched and cut--popping the buzzing things and severing a bit of his own tongue for the bargain.

"*Run!!*" The word came soaking in oily black blood, but Anders never knew if the woman heard.

The draugr were already inside--each feasting on the fresh, fear-seasoned meat they found. As fingers of the corrupted thing that had once been his lover gripped his neck, Anders Grendel knew them as the touch of pestilence. Lighter than straw and stronger than steel they were impossible to resist. All the man could do was hope that in the next world, his sins might be forgiven.

Before his vision failed, Anders turned to see the image of a young woman reaching out to him. She was holding something which flashed silver in the flickering light. Then he felt it, the cold touch of steel in his open hand. Only it wasn't steel. Bayla's *loves* had already devoured his eyes and tongue, but the man no longer needed them. Anders thrust forth the iron sheers as if they were the anointed sword of Saint George himself.

As iron pierced hide, the revolting horror that had been known as both Bayla and Esmé Grendel screamed along with every one of the revolting one-eyed bees. Though Bayla's heart was little more than paper and wax, it had long ago become the sort of thing that is bound by a very specific set of rules. As such, she could sense that the remaining moments were few and fleeting.

Shuddering in agony, the Grendel hive pulled closer the man that she had once loved in secret–a man who had once loved her in turn. And though Anders was already dead, the two shared one final kiss.

The buzzing things rained down. Each hitting the ground as oily liquid and as smoke.

Missy shielded herself, knowing that such things could not possibly be.

So she wiped her face and continued in her feverish task. While Anders had moved to confront the thing on the wall, Missy had begun wrapping her fiancé's neck with green pulp. The plantain leaves had been lifted from the Grendel's shed hours ago and were now freshly masticated. Of course Stewart would need immediate medical attention if tetanus was to be prevented, but that was okay.

Tetanus, she could deal with.

Missy spat out another wad of the chewed up leaves and applied them to the boy's arm. Having given up the sheers, there was no way to relieve the pressure in the sting there but she hoped for the best. With a grunt, she tore another sweat-soaked strip of her shirt away and wrapped the arm as tightly as she could.

It took some time to drag the bodies of the man and boy back to the previous chamber. They were both unconscious, but definitely alive. Only when both Stewart and Oscar lay by the old broken tree did Missy give herself a second to sit, lean back against the earthen wall and just breathe. In those long moments, her flesh hummed. Buzzing with fatigue and shock and far too many sanity-shattering events.

With a weak sigh, she looked up through the hole to see part of the moon. It was fully dark in the forest by Honning, Massachusetts, but for the first time in a very long time, silence reigned.

Just then, a tiny sound leaked out of the man she had treated first. The groan was weak but perhaps the most beautiful thing Missy had ever heard. She cupped the cheek of the man she loved, held his eyes in hers. Right then, she very much wanted to give all her remaining strength over to a well deserved cry. But it wasn't time for that.

"Stewart?" She moved the man's head onto her lap. "Can you hear me?"

The man winced, coughed, then went still again.

"Stewart!"

"Hmmm?" His voice was little more than a hiss. "Oh... hello darling." He offered a smile which was immediately and wholeheartedly returned. "Seems I tripped."

"Yes." Missy sniffed, wiped her eyes. "You really must watch your step."

"Is the boy...?"

"Here with us. His arm is broken but I think he'll be okay. You both will as soon as I get us out of this blasted hole and back to civilization." She looked up at the dangling ropes and the wooden rungs and remembered what Anders had said about putting the weight on top of her as she climbed.

"Darling?" Stewart's voice was small. "I can't remember... did we find anything worth writing about?"

"We certainly did. Volumes in fact." Missy's smile forced a tear to spill out onto her cheek. "Not that anyone is going to believe a word."

Stewart seemed to ponder this for a moment. Then he closed his eyes and said, "Well... a hundred years ago, no one believed in the platypus either."

Missy snorted, releasing a very long, very unladylike stream of mucus from one nostril. She clapped this away, glad that her fiancé's eyes were still closed. Leaning forward, she kissed the silly Blake-obsessed, would-be novelist whom she loved with all her heart.

As the moment lingered, the heat of it practically consumed her. It was many long seconds before she realized that Stewart Dunn had stopped kissing her back.

NO GOD BUT HUNGER

No God But Hunger

How many years had it been?

Remembering is hard but memories, however faded or fractured, are all we have. They've taken everything else. Everything real.

Blood drinkers, vampires, sasabonsam. When he was still alive, my uncle called them matsatsaku maza--the leech men. What they really were was an end. The end... and a beginning that no one asked for.

As the plague spread, so did things like panic, chaos and finally, a very long silence. Because after that, the only flies left upon the Earth's carcass were the ones who had learned a very hard lesson. Those little bugs knew better than to beat their tiny, buzzing wings. In other words--if what remained of mankind wanted to survive, he was going to have to crawl.

I can still remember that last night with Nico. In fact, if I concentrate hard enough... I can even smell the air. Sweet and a little spoiled. Like compost under a hot Tanzanian sun. Like meat that's gone to the worms.

Twenty-five. That's it. As of that night it had been twenty-five years since the world went red. Right before my world ended for the third time.

"Mirèlha."

My full name. I think he was the only one that used it anymore. I don't know why, but hearing it come out of that old Saffa's mouth always put me at full attention.

"The day is getting a bit on." He spoke in that familiar, almost jovial way he reserved for the people he liked best. "It would be smart to grass up. Maybe-maybe?"

Not wanting to, I looked down at my watch. The hands of the cartoon dog were at 9 and almost 4. Not quite 3:45pm, but I knew he was right.

"Fine," I turned to the expanse of savanna beside the road. With the animals who once grazed all extinct or nearly, the grass had grown to a height of around two meters. The blades ending in curled loops that swayed in the warm, late afternoon breeze.

"Better to come dressed for the party than to draw the host's eye."

"You made that one up, didn't you." I wasn't asking.

"Ja," Nico straightened up, both trying and failing to look important. "But I make all of them up. All the good ones anyway."

I think I just shook my head then. There we were, over nine hours into a full day of tracking with nothing to show for it but some new aches and a coat of freshly earned sweat. As it happened, I was not in the mood for one of Nico Bramsen's half-cooked proverbs.

Still... the man had a point.

There was something about the smell of death. Of decay. Like sharks, blood drew them close, but even the faintest trace of rot on the breeze was an affront to their heightened senses. Granted, walking around like living bushes was far from perfect camouflage, but it was something.

I jabbed the old oar I'd been carrying into the ground. The non-paddle end terminated in a sharp point I had whittled myself.

And so we began the process that Nico had shown me the previous summer. Plucking handfuls of the long grass and adding them to our ensembles. Inserting, tying, buckling them wherever trial and error had taught us were best. Off shoulders and behind the back. Hanging from our waist and strapped in great plumes to our forearms and legs until we looked like characters out of some nineteenth century jungle adventure story. King Solomon and the Restless Natives of Yukan-Fukoff-Tu.

"Nico."

"Ja?"

"Do you think there is an Italian restaurant left out there, somewhere?" I asked.

"What?" Nico sounded on the verge of a snicker. "I suppose it's possible. The cities belong to them, not us. And it's not like leeches eat people-food now do they. Why? You thinking spaghetti tonight?"

After affixing the last blade of grass to my Babanki mask, I fired off a sideways glare.

"No, dummy. If we can find some garlic, a couple of necklaces would be a hell of a lot more practical than all this."

"Oh ja. Garlic beats freshly plucked grass in the smell department, I grant you that." Nico shrugged. "But, we go to war with the weapons we have. Besides, you can't do this with a smelly necklace." He made a sweeping flourish with one arm. The grass tracing the movement into a low bow.

Of course I knew what he was doing. But like usual, I refused to give him the satisfaction of relinquishing his coveted prize. Such a little thing--a smile. And yet... still too damn expensive for the likes of Mirèlha Nanji.

If I could only go back... just hit control fucking Z and undo the last two decades.

"Yissus."

This, I remember him saying distinctly, for a sudden gravity had entered his tone. When I turned though, Nico wasn't looking at me.

"What is it?" I asked, my heart drumming in my throat. "What did you find?"

"Tracks," he said grimly--kneeling to inspect the ground. "Right there. Do you see?"

Though tracking has never been my forte, I bent over for a closer look. And to my surprise, I did see. "Too small to be a lion." I said with confidence. "God. Not a hyena... "

Nico scratched the line of his jaw. "It's the right size... but no. Look at the toes. They are two small, too separated. And see here?" He extended a finger close to the front of what I could absolutely see as toe prints. "No claws."

"Okay." Relieved, I straightened my back again. "And what does that mean?"

"It means we are tracking something that can hide its weapons when it moves."

"Damisa." I said, slipping into Hausa without meaning to.

"Yes," Said Nico with the beginnings of a wicked smile. "A leopard left this print. Those too. And unless I've gone cenile, it was carrying something in its mouth." He stood up and nodded at a patch of bare dirt less than a meter away. "Instinct is a powerful thing. For a leopard, it demands it carry any prey up into the branches of a tree. Leopards know that even if the current hunger is satisfied, there will soon be another... just around the bend. An insatiable God demanding yet another sacrifice." Nico paused for a few moments of silent contemplation before continuing. "One leopard can spend three days finishing a wildebeest or a zebra. Less if that prey is human."

Slowly, Nico turned to face me. In his eye was something primal, something of the wild. It reminded me that like everything else, we were predators too.

"There is no way of telling how far it has gone but these tracks were definitely made today. And... they go that way." He extended a finger. "East."

I looked in the indicated direction to see nothing but a sprawling sea of grass.

"Well." I said, scanning the plains ahead. "I don't see any trees. Do you?"

"No." Nico sounded like he wished there was more to say.

"Perhaps this particular cat has learned to adapt as we have? To live for the moment and finish its supper on the ground. Quickly--before night brings worse things."

I stared into the swaying grass--both hands tightening around my oar. I had also brought a long kitchen knife in my boot, but there was something about the oar that lent a degree of security. Nico was carrying his usual--that trusty garden hoe we found a few months back. In that rundown SDA church in Mkela. If the building hadn't been missing a wall, we never even would have checked it.

"Maybe," I went on. "The damned thing is listening to us right now. Waiting for the right moment."

"Maybe-maybe." Nico smiled thinly. "But tracks don't lie and neither does blood."

It was then I noticed the darker brown--flecks and slashes of it upon the dirt where we stood.

"This leopard has killed something for supper and is dragging it away. If not a tree, than somewhere else it feels safe." Nico's lips pursed in the way they always did when he was mulling over bad options. "If we turn back now, we will make it back to the canoe before the sun sets. On the way, we may even come across something to salvage this hunting trip. Who can say?"

"But..." I interjected. "These tracks are here now. A leopard, even a scrawny one, would feed our group for a few days if we are careful and ration properly. It would be a very good kill. But... there is another *but*." I let out a long breath. "Since there is no way of knowing how far the animal has gone, there's a chance, if we follow these tracks... we may not be getting any sleep tonight."

"Eloquently put, my China." Nico gave a mirthless chuckle. "Though I'd say that losing sleep is the least of our concerns. So... here is our dilemma. Do we press on, deeper into the lion's den? Or head back home and play it safe."

I responded with a grim nod. Then after consulting my plastic yellow watch, I took up the mask that hung from my belt. That old slab of wood, shaped long ago by the Babanki into something fierce. Something with curved tusks, a painted trunk and ugly vertical eyes. And like I did whenever I needed to become something other than myself, I slid the mask down. Hiding the woman. Becoming the beast.

"Safe?" I spoke with the confidence brought only by wearing my true face. "Safe is a dead concept."

For hours we moved across the Serengeti, checking every tree along the way. Carefully, systematically--always keeping one eye on the sun and its slow but steady descent. Though I did not yet regret my decision to go after the leopard, I was growing increasingly anxious. At my suggestion, more safety measures were added to our costumes. The yellow sap of the acacia tree smells a bit like bee honey, but it adds to the unappetizing qualities of our bouquet. We applied it in dots and lines to our faces and anywhere skin was showing. Then we kept going.

There were times I worried that Nico had lost the trail but then, there would be something--a print, some disturbed brush, or most encouraging of all... lines in the dirt which told us the animal was still dragging whatever it had killed. Finally, in the dying light, we saw something far more disturbing than the colors of the sky.

Signs of civilization.

"What do you think it is." I asked, looking at the collection of metal poles sticking straight up. There must have been twenty or more.

"I think..." Nico said thoughtfully. "It's a camp. Or it was."

For a second, I remained confused, but then it clicked. "Ah." I said, nodding. "The canvas roofs are probably long gone. I see. Those are the poles of some kind of campsite."

"Maybe-maybe." Nico didn't sound terribly interested. "Or one of those open air lodges? Way out in the bush for that authentic safari experience."

This caused the fingers around my sharpened oar to loosen. Civilization was a dangerous thing. Over the last twenty-five years, even the most meager of structures had been claimed. Four walls, a roof, something to block the windows, little more was required to escape the deadly rays of their great nemesis. In Predator World, the sun shone as brightly as ever, but the matsatsaku maza never saw it. For as Nico had said... by that particular point in history, the cities belonged to them.

"Well," I said with a sigh of relief. "Whatever that is or was, it doesn't look like a place for leeches."

"Nor for leopards, it would seem." Nico's eyes were on the ground, but they rapidly moved to the distance. Past the old campsite and to a very large acacia, maybe a kilometer away. "Do you see the part in the grass? There. Right there."

I peered out the eye slits of my mask.

"That's the one." He said with a hint of excitement.

"But... we've passed so many trees. Why would this leopard come so far?"

To my surprise, Nico said nothing. At least at first.

"Home is home, my China." He smiled, showing that I was not the only one wearing a cracked mask.

"Nico," I placed a hand on his shoulder--looked down at a man slightly shorter than myself. "It's 6:21. The sun will be down in less than thirty minutes.

If that's our tree, I would like to finish this."

After a few silent moments, he looked up. "Yes," He said. "The lizard who considers the road for too long, may get paved over before ever taking a step."

"If you say so." I shook my head.

Making sure to stay low to the ground, the two of us set off, moving as quickly as possible. As we came to the big acacia, our pace slowed. The lowest branch had to be fifteen meters from the ground. but there was no sign of any leopard. At least not to my eyes.

"This is it." Nico was whispering. "Look at the bark!"

I didn't know what he was talking about. The sun was almost set and we were still moving.

"I see a tree."

"Is that all?" Even whispering there was an insidious smile in Nico's voice.

"Yes, damn it. I--"

I stopped--talking, moving... everything but looking. I reached out to the irregular surface of the acacia's trunk, and that's when I realized that portions of it had been clawed away. I turned to Nico, then gazed up into the branches. I couldn't see, hear or smell the beast but by God, I knew it was up there.

"The best way to catch a leopard is to find where it lives. If it's not home, just climb up and wait. I guarantee you will be the last thing it will expect to find in its parlor."

"Yeah?" I said, still staring up into the dark, canopy shadows. "And what if it is home?"

"Well..." Nico was taking out a length of rope from his pack. With one hand, he swung it around the trunk--catching the end with his other. "Then you are definitely going to piss it off," He flipped the rope a ways up the trunk. "In that case, it is best to have someone on the ground with strong arms... because they may very well need to catch you."

"Can you do me one favor?" I asked. "Can that one be the last proverb of the day?"

"What proverb? I'm being completely literal." Nico pulled himself a bit higher up the tree, before digging in his heels and repeating the process. "Just hold onto that oar. And if something falls that isn't me, I want you to hit it on the head. Hard and a lot."

"Don't worry about me, Saffa. Just pay attention to what you're--"

A low noise drifted down from above. It was a warning. A growl wrapped in a hiss. It stopped my mouth from flapping, my heart from beating. And though it felt as if I were moving in slow motion, I inclined my head up, up, once more into the pitch dark shadows of the acacia... just in time to see two yellow eyes.

I raised my weapon but not fast enough. The leopard dropped or pounced--from that height it hardly mattered. Nico had been right--the animal was undeniably pissed off. The initial impact felt more like someone had dropped a water buffalo on me than a 30 kilo cat. I lifted my weapon, but the force was too much.

I felt the snap as if it had been one of my bones that had broken in two.

After that, the world was replaced with horrible yellow teeth. My hands flew instinctively to my hard, wooden face--each gripping a piece of what had once been a canoe oar. I thought it was all over. Any second, my skin would be raked by claws, or my throat would feel a vice-like pressure of the leopard's kiss. I think it was then that I began to feel we had made the wrong decision. Gone the wrong way. We could have gone home. Could have been safe.

Safe?

In that moment, as I realized the hot breath in my nostrils was not my own--I remembered this was bullshit. There was no such thing as safe. In Predator World, there was only this. That which had replaced God. The question was, who was more hungry? The cat? Or the crazy bitch in the elephant mask?

My face shot forward, resulting in an impact that registered as a flash behind my eyes. I had smashed the leopard right in the mouth, causing it to rear back, just enough. Needing to capitalize, my right hand stabbed down, still gripping wood. The thrust was all and everything I had. It wasn't enough to puncture the leopard's hide, but the gasping shriek as I stabbed that broken piece of oar into its throat was music. It told me I had hurt the thing.

I tried to roll away, but a large paw came down on my chest and slammed me back to the ground. Then, powerful legs were all around, as a spotted hide became the sky.

I remember screaming. Beating the heavy thing on top of me with alternating pieces of broken oar. Wanting to deal out more pain, but even my strongest hits were glancing, feeble things. I was weak and pathetic and worst of all, I was going to die looking like a damned fool. Nico's grass could do nothing to protect me from anything as natural as a leopard.

"Get off! Get off!" I roared in impotent outrage--thoroughly underwhelmed with what might be my final words.

The teeth had returned. Curved and long and yellow. Past them, radiated the heat of a thousand suns but the thing's reeking breath was like smelling salts--steeling my waning nerve. I fought and I pushed and I continued to scream. Dreading, more than anything, that inevitable moment when the cat's claws would find my flesh. And though uninvited, would proceed to enter me.

"Ha!!"

The impact came from the side. The metal head of a garden hoe was jabbed so hard into the cat's side, I heard a dull cracking. I tried to see what was happening, but everything swam. With a sharp inhalation, I scrambled to my feet. And though I knew Nico was battling for both his life and mine, something in me went soft. Both of my hands opened--letting the two halves of oar fall and bounce off the ground.

My hands flew over my body then--searching for new openings, finding none. And as I stood there, hugging myself, wanting to weep out of rage and violation, I felt the pain of a very old scar. Unable to stop myself, one hand began to travel behind my shoulder--suddenly needing to touch. To feel the raised skin of the letters that had been carved there.

"*Mirèlha*!!" The sound of my name pulled me back to the moment. "*We have to be quick! End this, now!*"

I looked with wide, startled eyes. Nico and the leopard were facing each other. The cat, snarling, baring long teeth and considerable fury. Nico had switched to the other end of his garden hoe. The vampire-killing end--sharpened to a long point in the fashion of my late oar. This was a shocking thing to see. After all, it was Nico who loved reminding me that a smart kill was one with no blood spilled. It was the safe play. The reason he always chose to brain animals with the dull, metal end of that hoe. Because blood brings blood.

"If it runs into the grass, we won't be able to track it till morning!"

I looked out across the savanna, which was now almost completely dark.

"We have to get in front of it, " I began, shakily. "Put the tree to its back!"

Out of my left boot, I retrieved the kitchen knife. Then the two of us began sidestepping until the animal we had tracked for so many hours had nowhere to go. In the moonlight, its eyes flashed with unholy light. It was snarling and spitting and then... it wasn't.

The change that came over the leopard was instantaneous. Lips fell, covering the teeth. Ears shot straight back to lie flat against the skull. The animal's rage was inexplicably gone--replaced by what I could only describe as fear.

Fear, yes... but not for us.

As I looked again into those darkened plains, I saw that the leopard was staring straight at the site we had passed. That collection of poles that stuck straight up in the air that had once been a camp, or lodge, but could not possibly offer shelter for something like the matsatsaku maza.

The noises were distant at first. A faint, high-pitched snarling that I recognized at once. Then the grass between us and the vertical poles began to rustle. Whatever was coming was moving fast and low to the ground.

"Mirèlha."

I heard my name distantly, as if in a dream.

"Take this."

The leopard was forgotten as was the knife in my hand. In that moment, all I could do was stare at the unseen death rustling through the grass, coming straight for us.

"*Damn it, woman!*"

That time, Nico's voice came with a physical component. The handle of his garden hoe was pressing into me--lengthwise across my chest.

"I can't do this alone."

Finally I turned to him. To my partner. My friend. The first I had made in a very long time. Then I pushed the garden implement back towards him.

"You don't have to." I said, kneeling to pick up a piece of broken oar from the ground. The movement caused the leopard to hiss at me before scrambling out and away--disappearing into the dark savanna.

"Shit," I said with a sneer.

"Forget the cat." Nico had his battle hoe up and ready. "We'll find it again. Carry its carcass back to Jua and then eat like kings and queens."

From behind my mask, I snickered. "Providing we survive the next few minutes, you mean?"

"Minutes?" Nico was smiling. "Think this will last so long?"

"Maybe-maybe." I said without meaning to. The set of weapons felt strange and wrong, but I had survived with less. Still, I couldn't stop wondering if I should lead with the kitchen knife or the broken piece of wood. But after another second passed, the grass parted and I had something else to think about.

The matsatsaku maza were utterly hairless--their skin a perfect pitch black. But this only served to accentuate certain other features. The white teeth, the talon-like nails and those hideous eyes--solid red like whole cherries. All these things flashed, but Nico and I stood our ground. For with their emergence came a small measure of relief. These four, were the small kind. The sort of monster that still approximated the size and shape of men... or in this case, children.

If I had to guess, none had been more than fifteen when they last felt the sun on their backs. And though I knew they were all far older than they appeared, it was difficult to trick my eyes.

I had fought and killed others like them before... but it had not been easy.

"Get the cat."

The pack's alpha was a girl, I quickly realized. She spoke Swahili, but never more than a few words at a go. Though I wasn't fluent, I managed to keep up.

"Take it home," She hissed. *"We will follow."*

Something like that.

I watched as two broke from the rest and vanished into the outer-dark. Right then I felt a great swell of outrage in my chest. They were going after the leopard.

Our fucking leopard.

I knew that a single bite was all it would take to infect the meat. And that thought at that particular moment made me very angry. No--angry isn't the word. We had to make this quick. Live through the next few seconds, but we also had to get that leopard. The muscles in my arms brimmed with frustrated, potential energies. And when the moment finally came, my body shot forward, straight past Nico, straight for the leader.

As I rushed, she stood there unconcerned. As if an errant breeze was coming her way instead of a crazy masked Ugandan.

I think I heard my name but it was too late for thought. Too late for anything to stop a knife which was already thrusting down. Even so, the little bitch didn't move. I can still feel her eyes and that ever widening, piranha-smile, searing into my retinas. Right then, I didn't know what was making her so damned confident... but I learned.

Three more appeared from the grass. Hitting me in the side like a careening truck. Adding their weight to the two already standing by her side as they slammed me to the ground. Even a single young leech is a dangerous thing and right then, I had a dog-pile of five to contend with.

In frustration more than anything, I screamed obscenities in their faces. For there I was again--on my back, struggling in vain, helpless, waiting for the end. I could feel them gripping my arms and neck and legs. Reaching down with little hooked fingers, giggling their insidious liquid giggles.

Les enfants infernaux. That was the phrase that popped into my mind as I lay buried. Something my mother might have said.

"*Little shits!*" The voice of Nico Bramsen roared--piercing the ravening hiss like a choir of fucking angels. "*You get off of her!*"

One shrieked, leaving my ears ringing. There was a surge in the crushing weight and then, some much needed relief as two from the pile above were pulled away. I gasped to regain some of my lost air, then looked to my right. Nico's homemade spear had gone all the way through the first one's heart and into the ribs of the second. That was the one who had shrieked in my ear and it was shrieking still. The three still on top of me were distracted. Seizing the moment, I thrust my knife forward, plunging it directly into one of their chests. Then I reached out and pulled the screaming thing toward me--squeezing until I saw the point of the blade stick out of its back.

As it happens, the stories got a few things right. Sun burns, garlic repels and the heart is always the spot you aim for. Thing is, the killing blow can be delt with a consecrated stake of white oak, a kitchen knife or pretty much anything else, as long as it goes *all the way through.*

The body of the leech slumped down, covering me like a shroud. It was dead. I had killed something that looked a lot like a child. But I couldn't think of it like that. Had to keep reminding my eyes that they were lying. That however this creature appeared, it was a predator. And more importantly... our competition.

With a great surge of effort I was able to get free and back on my feet. Adrenaline coursing, I swung the piece of wood in my hand. The broken oar whistled and then it smashed one of the leech kids in the face!

"The leader's gone!" From the sound of Nico's voice I could tell he was actively fighting. "Looks like she's going back to that campsite--or whatever the hell it used to be."

Nico finished off the one he was fighting and I turned to the one I had hit. It was rubbing its jaw, looking afraid... or at least, uncertain. It was a boy, or at least, had been. Maybe eight or nine when turned.

"I think she sent the others after the leopard." I shouted without taking my eyes off the boy that wasn't. "As alpha, they might wait for her to eat first, but our leopard will be torn apart in seconds. We can't let that happen."

"Agreed." Out of breath, Nico stepped to my side.

United, we stared down the last of them--les enfants infernaux. Watching as those solid cherry-like eyes flitted between us and the dark unknown. It looked like a little bird that wanted to fly. And despite everything I knew, everything I had seen and done to survive since the world went red... right then, there was only one thing I wanted.

"Fly, little bird. Fly away and don't look back."

It's funny the bits that come back, and the ones that never do.

When I try, I can not summon the name of my first professor... or the way my mother smelled when she gave me that last hug before bed. But after Nico and I killed the last of the baby leeches, when ran for those poles... I can still remember the wind. How cool it felt on my hot, blood-spattered skin.

Upon reaching the campsite, it was clear that Nico had been right about that too. The place had been one of those open air lodges, complete with the skeletons of eight tents that had surely once catered to a special breed of tourist.

Between the poles were piles of various things I could not identify. Some items, like broken chairs and other furniture, had probably been part of the lodge. Others looked to be personal belongings. Packs and clothes, even things that might be used as weapons. Then there were the bones. Animal and human alike. Thousands of them, gleaming in the light of the moon. Collected by earth's newest apex and placed in tribute to that which had become their God.

"Maybe there's something here we can use." I said, approaching a long wooden pole sticking out of one pile. I had lost my knife in the last tussle and had only the broken oar to defend myself with. "Do you see her? The leader?"

"No." Nico said, circling the naked tents, checking to make sure the alpha wasn't hiding behind.

"This makes no sense," I said, pulling on the pole, hoping for something the length of a quarterstaff I could whittle into a point. "Leeches need four walls, a roof--and even then they black out the windows." I pulled again, harder this time. "How can there be a nest here? There is nowhere to hide."

"Well..." Having checked the last of the roofless tents, Nico leaned on his garden hoe. "I have heard stories of leeches doing strange things. There was a man I knew, in Mozambique. Raul claimed to have come upon one of them, just as the sun was about to rise. It was lying there--dead, he thought... then it turned its head. After that, he stood frozen in place, just waiting for the rosy fingers of dawn to turn the damned thing to ash."

I stopped what I was doing then. Just listened.

"Appearing quite unconcerned, the leech apparently put its head back down. And, just as the sun's light was about to reach it, the thing did something my friend Raul had not expected. It melted. Right into the earth."

"Melted?" I repeated the word, unconvinced. "Right into the earth?"

"That's how he described it," Said Nico with a shrug. "Or that the very dirt beneath, somehow reached up to make the monster a part of itself. To protect it from the harsh light of morning, almost like a sort of cocoon."

"Huh," I said flatly. "Sounds like Raul didn't have both his oars in the water."

Nico snickered. "You may be right. But as we both know... just because something has never been seen before does not make it fiction."

I relinquished a nod then. My mind drifted back to those early news reports--to the rampant jokes and tweets and posts that made believing the impossible even harder.

"Dirt cocoons." I said soberly--knowing that I had no right or reason to disbelieve a damn thing. "You really think that's what's happening here?"

"Me?" Nico poked at an overturned chair with the toe of his boot. "Heck, I'm just making conversation."

With a sigh, my hands returned to the wooden pole--gripping as tight as they could. Then, mustering one final pull, the thing came loose! Unable to stop myself, I stumbled back. My heart was racing as I looked at my hard-won prize. The tip of the spear was solid steel, maybe thirty five centimeters long. Sturdy, relatively free of rust. I thrust the weapon forward in the air--once and again.

"Yeah," I said. "This will do." Just then, my foot stepped on something that wasn't earth. Looking down, I moved my foot in an arc--sweeping some of the dirt away. "Nico, look. There are boards here. I think it's a deck or some kind of patio."

Though the light was low, once we knew what to look for, the repeating parallel lines were hard to miss. The boards had been set directly into the ground. My eyes followed them around two of the tents. Then I saw it. The ultimate amenity one looks for when booking an authentic trip to adventure away from the world of modern convenience.

"Well I'll be damned." Nico's voice dripped with disdain as much as wonder. "It's a pool."

"Of course. What else?" I said with a snicker. "You can't get that authentic safari experience without a swimming pool."

With practiced caution, I approached the edge of the deep, rectangular hole and glared down. The old pool was lined with concrete and tile but it held no water--only what appeared to be a number of huge, crumpled tarps.

"Dirt cocoons, eh?" I said with far too much sarcasm. "More like the roofs to all these tents. Still, that must have taken some real ingenuity. Finding this place and seeing a potential home."

"Home..." His tone had a distant, thinking-out-loud quality. "Home is where you make it... where you find your bread and break it."

"Don't think these kids are living on bread, Nico."

He laughed then, but it was thin--automatic. The eyes of the old Saffa were pointing past the pool at the coming pair of pitch-black forms rushing toward us. One of them had something over its shoulder. Something tawny and covered in spots.

At that point, I swore in Hausa. Can't remember what I said exactly, but I'm sure it was colorful.

The pair who had been sent after the leopard were returning to discover they had a couple of uninvited guests in their parlor. At a distance of perhaps ten meters, I could see that the two leeches had only three eyes between them. Suddenly, the one I've come to think of as Tall Boy hurled his prize--the limp body of the leopard sliding in the dirt, rolling until it came to a stop by one of the tent poles. It was dark and as only a second was spared to look, I couldn't tell if the animal was dead or just stunned.

The shorter of the two leeches was missing an eye. That one was the first to lunge and was the first to be cut down. First, Nico delivered a hard jab with the flat of the garden hoe's head. Then he pivoted--swinging with centrifugal force, burying the edge into the meat of One Eye's right side. It screamed. And then it didn't. Though I had seldom seen him use it, the edge of Nico's trusty hoe had been sharpened to a razor. After pulling back the weapon, the old Saffa lashed out again with that sharpened edge. Separating the still wailing head of One Eye from its post.

Preoccupied as he was, Nico didn't see the next attack coming. Didn't know that his actions had sent Tall Boy charging with outstretched arms that looked too long on its frame. Fortunately, Nico was not alone. He had Mirèlha Nanji for a partner. A girl who, once upon a time, had chosen javelin over table tennis as her sport of choice. It had been years since I'd thrown, but there was no time to waste remembering how. My arm and eye remembered how to aim. My hand, just when to release.

The spear whistled as it flew. And then it didn't. And though my strike missed the heart, it gave Nico ample time to spin round and thrust with the stake end of his weapon. Finishing the lanky, slathering Tall Boy off in one, well placed strike that went all the way through.

I looked at Nico and he looked back. Both of us were out of breath. Both covered in blood that was not our own. For a second, I thought we were done. But there was something pulling at my attention. A rustling sort of sound, drawing my eye, down, down into the deep, rectangular hole in the ground. To the crumpled mass of tarps which I could now tell, were moving.

My heart skipped. My fingers desperately clutching for the weapon I had already thrown.

"Mirèlha!"

I turned to see that Nico had already hurled my spear. My hand reached out, catching the moving shaft in mid-flight. I began lifting the weapon but the arm brandishing it was promptly pinned in a position that denied leverage. The alpha leech had leapt out of the pool and was on me, above me, everywhere! Its legs wrapped around and under my arms, squeezing, forcing the air from my lungs! Though it weighed very little, the strength of that damned little leech was enormous. And with every step I stumbled backward, its gaping mouth moved closer and closer.

I remember the teeth. How white they looked in the moonlight. How perfect. Like slivers of solid pearl.

One hand shot free and without a second's hesitation, I drove a thumb deep into the left eye of my attacker. There came a shriek and an incredible relief of pressure. Finally, with the damn thing off me, I could breathe.

I lashed out--jabbing with with the spear. This new extension of myself. It was my claws. My rage.

My first strike skewered the throat of the child-shaped thing I could find no pity for. The alpha seemed dazed. Its remaining eye, wide and red with surprise. It looked as if it wanted to speak or just beg, maybe.

Maybe-maybe.

Before it could do any of that, I yanked on the spear, then plunged it into the thing's heart.

I remember how I felt then. Breathing, standing there amidst those naked tents and bones and piles of collected treasure with the inky blood of the alpha on my skin. I lifted the Babanki mask and swept my eyes over the camp. Then I looked at my friend. Nico looked tired and maybe, older than either he or I wanted to admit.

Like he had done so many times before, the old Saffa offered me a smile. And though I did not return it, I did allow myself to feel triumphant. To believe that, just for one damn second, we were safe. I should have remembered that safe is a dead concept. Had been for twenty five years. Sure, les enfants infernaux were all slain... but I had forgotten about the leopard.

It all happened so fast. First I saw movement in the shadows. Then a flash of color.

I cannot say when the animal had awakened, only that it did not waste the quiet moment. Its attack was well planned, well timed. The leopard struck fast, sinking its teeth into the throat of Nico Bramsen.

I can remember wanting to scream and to vomit. To lash out with my spear--to rip the spotted devil apart with my bare hands. By God, I wanted to do all of it. But I didn't. Couldn't. I was frozen--bewitched by those yellow eyes. The very same I first saw up in the shadowy branches of an old acacia.

And so I watched, gaping in horror as my friend was dragged away. As the animal we had tracked for most of a day pulled at his already limp form and then, began to run. Disappearing into the grass and the long, merciless hours of night.

Yes--remembering is hard, but it is also important.

However painful, I remember that last night with Nico as if it was yesterday. In fact, if I concentrate hard enough... I can even smell the air. Sweet and a little spoiled. Like compost under a hot Tanzanian sun. Like meat that's gone to the worms.

It reminds me of how much we've lost. Of how much has been sacrificed at the altar of the only God this world worships.

For me that night was far from over.

Once the leopard was out of sight, control of my body returned to a woman who was utterly shattered, but who was also filled with enough rage to fill a mountain. Revenge was all I wanted. I needed it. Hungered for it.

And so, after consulting my plastic yellow watch, I reached up to the mask again. That old slab of wood, shaped long ago by the Babanki into something fierce. Something with curved tusks, a painted trunk and ugly vertical eyes. And like I did whenever I needed to become something other than myself, I slid the mask down. Hiding the woman. Becoming the beast.

GROWTH
JUST

Growing Just Beneath

"Your tree is screwed."

The statement through me for a loop. I was still loading some cans of soda into the fridge when my aunt and uncle walked through the front door. We were hosting a low key summer barbecue and as usual they were the first to arrive. I looked up, not entirely sure I had heard correctly.

"What's that?" I said.

"The dogwood out there. It's screwed." My uncle was shaking his head "Did you know?"

I stood up--glanced out the kitchen window. Along with the house and the *expansive* quarter acre lot, a number of gardens and flower beds became ours when my wife and I signed on the dotted line. The gardens themselves were actually quite nice and seemed well tended, as far as I could tell. But then, what do I know? Most of the flowers I can name are the ones I knew at the end of third grade. Roses, daisies--I'm pretty sure that tulips are the ones with the three points on top that look like Bart Simpson hair.

That said, even someone with my limited botanical knowledge would know our one tree was a dogwood.

"Screwed? What does *that* mean?" I asked almost defensively. "What's wrong with it?"

"It has been invaded." My uncle looked sympathetic then. Like he was about to admit to running over the cat. "You, my friend, have bittersweet."

The declaration hung between us like a cloud--pregnant with storms which had not arrived yet, but would very soon. To me, bittersweet was something you said when you're first-born moves away to college. It was an adjective. What my seven year old still calls, a *describer*. How can one *have* bittersweet? It was like saying the Bruins *had triumphant* after winning game seven of the Stanley Cup playoffs.

Reading the question on my face, my uncle smiled. "Come on. I'll show you." And without another word, the two of us exited the kitchen and then the house.

Having arrived at the tree, my eyes searched and scoured. As far as I was concerned, nothing looked out of place. Sure it didn't bloom like the ones on Main street and yes, the thing was inexplicably split down the center--thus resembling a child's rendering of water spouting from the top of a cartoon whale... but there were plenty of leaves. All green and healthy and thriving.

A fact which, as I would soon learn, was precisely the problem.

As it happened, competing on my tree were two distinct types of leaf. Amidst the dogwood's own, another had asserted itself. Somewhat longer with fierce points and serrated edges. The more I stared, the more out of place these other leaves appeared. Slowly, my eyes moved to a conspicuous group of berries--some were orange, others red. Were dogwoods supposed to have berries? All I knew was the tiny spheres were pulling branches on both sides--splitting my tree in twain.

I was equal parts outraged and appalled. Affronted by an attack upon something for which I suddenly felt a great swell of affection for. These leaves, these berries, they were features of a single villain. An evil parasite which sought only to devour and destroy its helpless host. Gripped by something I can only describe as anger, my eyes traced the vines all the way down to the ground. Right to the source.

There, hidden in plain sight. I saw my true enemy for the first time. A twisted, spiraling thing. like some unholy amalgamation of chameleon and snake was the mother root. Without eyes she glared back--utterly confident in her ability to continue on unmolested. I had never looked upon anything so vile. So utterly alien. In that moment, I wanted to hack at the twisted thing--to tear it away with my bare hands.

"Oh yeah. That's it right there." Said my uncle, sounding like a vindicated Sherlock Holmes. "That's where all this mess started." He was pointing right at her. Right at the *mother*. "Friggin' bittersweet. I tell ya--we've got it in the woods behind our house. You leave this crap alone long enough and it'll take over every time."

As I listened, my angst got the better of me. I scowled at my newfound enemy, then gave it a firm tug... but the mother root wouldn't budge.

"Now listen." My uncle went on in the confident tone of an older man imparting his years of hard-earned experience. "You gotta pull all this down." He gestured to the branches above. To the leaves and the bright alien spheres. "But lay down a tarp first. Let the berries fall on that instead of the ground. You gotta think of this crap as the plant equivalent of a starfish. Leave behind a single berry or strand of root, it's just gonna grow right back. And it'll *keep* growing."

As he spoke, I nodded and absorbed. Even then, I was unsure that my outrage would last long enough to see these instructions through but, I hoped it would. I really did. Maybe for the first time, I found that I actually wanted to be one of those *responsible homeowner types*. A character like you'd see in some bad sitcom--who describes the contents of their weekend on Monday mornings as a series of outdoor labors. Mowed the lawn... finished the retaining wall... rescued my dogwood from a horrible parasitic plant monster...

"Alright," I said with resolve. "If I get it all... do you think the tree will recover?"

My uncle stepped back. He looked the dogwood over again, from stem to stern, considering the question.

"Maybe. As long as you get it all but, that's the trick." Then he gave a quick scan to the surrounding lawn. "See these?" He was kneeling before an unassuming weed--little more than a thin green sprout and some leaves. *Tiny, serrated leaves.* "These things are the real problem. Everything up on that tree is because of one of these little shits."

I reached for the nearest sprout, ready to tear it away with extreme prejudice.

"Wouldn't do that." My uncle was holding his hands up in a very *don't look at me* sort of way. "If you pull on that now, you're gonna be out here all day. Trust me, come back when you've got some time. When you're ready for a fight. I know they don't look like much, but these things have roots like you wouldn't believe. Bright copper, the color of new pennies. Instead of making a little root cluster, they only move down a few inches beneath the dirt before banging a hard left. From there they shoot out, pretty much parallel to the surface. It's ridiculous. Just one of these things will infect your whole yard and you have way more than one."

I scanned the grass around us--taking in all the insidious sprouts while still not fully comprehending the severity of the situation. Bizarrely, my subconscious began to regurgitate a scene from a nature documentary I had seen. I could recall a segment on the garden eel--a tiny black and white fish that buries itself, tail first, in the sand. When there are no predators around, these eels will extrude their bodies from the earth and simply hang there, just swaying with the current.

As I looked at the army of tiny invaders, sticking up from the grass and soil, I wondered if they might retract at my approach. In that moment I felt surrounded, but also something like a predator. Some prehistoric, deep sea shark. Bittersweet had become my prey and now that I knew the myriad faces it wore, I could see nothing else.

The next day was Sunday.

I awoke, staring at the cracked plaster ceiling of the master bedroom. I hadn't slept well.

Beside me, my wife lay sleeping and I moved carefully so as not to disturb her. No reason for anyone else to get up so early, but for me there was little choice. Now that the gears had started turning, my options were either: get on with the day or keep studying the cracks in the ceiling.

Moving downstairs, my footsteps were plodding, clumsy. Halfway down, I glanced out the window at the front yard. In that moment, through the haze of new wakefulness, I saw my tree for what felt like the first time. God, it looked so broken. Split in half, like the peel from a half-naked banana. As I stared, my frustration grew. I was annoyed at the situation--at the amount of work ahead of me, but more than anything, I was pissed that the plight of my own damn tree had to be pointed out to me. Up until the previous day, I had accepted the dogwood as I saw it, pockmarks and all. And for three years the bittersweet had grown without impedance.

"Time to pay the reaper."

Even as I said this, I knew the line was off. That I was mincing quotes somehow. But... it was too early to think. Right then I needed coffee. Coffee and gloves.

The battle commenced just before 8:30 am that day. I decided to take my uncle's advice, but without a big enough tarp, I used the cover from our pool. Laid it down in front and around the trunk, securing it with a number of medium-sized rocks. Finally, with the morning sun keeping watch, I set about my task.

Inspecting a cluster of berries, I located what looked like the end of one of the creeper vines. It was wrapped around a large branch like thread around a spool. This, I carefully unwound and pulled. Pulled until stars appeared in the morning sky. At first it seemed a futile effort but after a second or two, the branch gave up about three inches of vine.

I jolted back from the sudden slack. My heart was pounding. Soaring. I knew the feeling was disproportionate to the amount of progress that had been made, but I didn't care. My eyes devoured the branches, then moved to the grass below. To the tiny soldiers standing there. The invading army of garden eels which stood at attention. I reminded myself that there were two battles to be fought. One above the earth and another just beneath. Undaunted by the breadth of my task, I tightened my grip and launched back into the fray.

My hands moved by as if themselves. Ripping. Tearing. Unseating. Liberating. The alien parasites were all I saw, *all I knew*. Time was no longer a consideration. My younger daughter appeared at one point, but I didn't stop. Couldn't stop. Acknowledging her only distantly, through a whirlwind of branch and leaf and fury.

When the task was done, I looked up to see that the pale morning sky had been replaced by a royal blue, afternoon one. I stepped back, needing to view my Impressionist masterpiece the proper way--from a distance. But as I moved, I became aware of thin lines of pain all over my skin. Sweat was leaking into a dozen cuts I hadn't felt until that moment, but the pain was good. Justified. Earned. As for the tree--*my tree...* it looked positively anorexic. Nearly one fifth of its previous bulk now lay on a pool cover I could hardly see anymore. The war was ongoing, yes, but the first battle had been won. I alone stood victorious--the Reaper.

And in that moment, *I had triumphant.*

"Jesus Christ!" Exclaimed my wife. "What the hell happened to *you?*"

By then I had trudged into the house. Exhausted but with an amazing amount of satisfaction, I recounted the day's battle.

"What time is it?" I asked suddenly aware of a powerful thirst.

"Two forty-eight!" Came the voice of my youngest "I told you lunch was ready *four times*, but I don't think you heard. You just kept yelling at that tree."

"Here." My wife approached setting down a glass and a plate containing what looked like a cold version of one of her famous maple chicken paninis. "Come here. Let me see." She began to inspect my various lacerations making me feel less *triumphant* and more *little kid who just fell off his bike.* But it was fine. All was well. I was done and for now at least, I had a sandwich.

"Is the tree gonna be okay, Daddy?"

Mouth full of maple-flavored chicken, I smiled.

"I fink fo." I took three giant gulps from the glass, almost emptying it. "But, Daddy's not done yet."

"Not done?!" Exclaimed my youngest, launching into hyperbole. "You were already out there for a million years, today! How come you're not done?"

I smiled.

"Jeez. Some of these cuts are kind of bad." My wife sounded concerned, running a gentle thumb over my arm. "Didn't you feel them?"

I thought on this. Thought and chewed and thought some more.

"Honestly? No. Not even one." I said. "I guess I was in the zone."

My wife looked up with a sardonic eyebrow. "I *guess.* We saw the pile from the window. Can't believe how much of the tree, *wasn't tree!*" She shook her head sympathetically. "So, what's left to do?"

"Well..." I said with a sigh. "Apparently bittersweet spreads like a virus. I took care of what was up in the branches... but there's more. These ittle sprouts with roots that bang hard lefts." I shrugged. "I don't know--I wanted to clear off my tree first."

"*Your* tree?" Her tone was playful. A parody of affrontation.

"*The* tree." I made a show of sounding as annoyed as I possibly could. "Anyway, I think I'll take a break and then go out again later." With one more gulp I finished the lemonade. "Hopefully it won't take too much longer." I moved in for a kiss knowing full well how filthy I was.

"Yeah right." My wife stepped away, tossing me a smirk.

"Alright, alright." I said, turning to go upstairs. "Shower, good. Dirt, bad. I get it. Thanks for the sandwich."

"Sure..." Her voice trailed off. Then she came up quickly behind me. "Hold on a second." Gently, she put hands on my arm and shoulder.

"What?" I said. "Do I have some squashed berries on me or something?"

"...*Something.*" She sounded strange. "Ooh, man--how'd I miss this? Does it hurt when I do *this?*"

My reaction was explosive. It felt like she was measuring the depth of an open wound with a toothpick.

"Ah! *Yes!* What are you--?"

"Hold still." She said. Her tone was clinical now. My jaws clicked shut, clenching in pain.

"*What the fuck?!*" I jabbed back, immediately regretting it. "Sorry--I didn't mean..." When I looked, my wife was staring at something in her hand.

"Gross." She said, sounding more fascinated than anything. "It looks like a little worm."

The thing was about four inches long. Brittle looking but supple to the touch. It was bright copper, the color of new pennies.

"Actually, I think it's a little root." She finished the thought, turning the thing over in her palm. "This thing was *really in there.*"

I never made it back out to my tree that day. Nor the next. In fact, three weeks passed before I was able to gather enough will to once again face the Goddamned bittersweet. By then, most of my cuts had healed and faded into nonexistence. All except the one behind my shoulder. It was that cut my finger was tracing as I stood there, surrounded by dozens of innocuous looking sprouts.

These things are the real problem. I could hear the voice of my uncle. *Everything up on that tree is because of one of these little shits.*

I knew enough to be gentle and the first sprout was lifted easily. But as I continued to pull--gently, slowly, I saw that my uncle had not exaggerated. Bit by bit, the soil began to pop. Like tiny firecrackers going off beneath the grass-- all of them in a straight line. Each pop came with a puff of fine dirt and another inch or more of coppery root. It was unbelievable. After a short while, almost an entire foot of the stuff connected the tiny green sprout in my hand to the underground. And the more I extracted, the more I wanted. On my brow was a fever. One that could only be cured by ridding the soil of its affliction. For that too was mine--the very soil along with the tree and every blade of grass.

It was all so clear. So simple. I was the Reaper once again, and by God I would not stop until the harvest was done. The insidious roots had become my nemesis. Every time I thought I was coming to the end of one section, another branch would appear. They were circuits, vast neural pathways, coppery rivers with tributaries uncountable and they were growing--always growing just beneath.

By the time I stopped to breathe, the lawn had been transformed. Around me, where green grass had flourished only hours before, stretched a patchwork of great brown scars. My heart raced, my muscles hummed and the unhealed cut on my shoulder throbbed in time. No quarter had been given, no mercy shown. I looked around for some sign of the sprouts. Those tiny green soldiers that had possessed gaul enough to flank my tree on all sides. But these were gone, slain. Every one, reaped with extreme prejudice.

A trembling hand extracted a phone, checked the time. 5:39 PM. *Damn.* I had been at if for over six hours. Hadn't even stopped for lunch. Not even a glass of water. I tried to remember if anyone had come out--my wife, my youngest. Perhaps to offer these things at some point. It seemed likely, but I could remember nothing beyond the fight. In my mind, the afternoon was a blur. A maelstrom of popping dirt and miles of bright copper lines.

I turned for the house, but before I took a step, a thought sparked in my brain. It was like an alarm I had set and then forgotten about. I couldn't go inside because I wasn't done. Not yet. Not with one battle left to fight. I turned to regard the trunk of my tree, and there she was, glaring right back--the source. She who had begotten all of my recent woes. The mother root. The alien queen.

I approached slowly, unable to look away. Unlike all her children, the flesh of my true enemy had faded to an ashen grey. A thought occurred at this. Perhaps she was dead already. Perhaps the war *was* over after all. I gripped her form, though gently. She was very old and, somehow I knew, very much alive. Whatever else she deserved, the mother root had my respect.

The initial tug was exploratory. Then, respect or no, my efforts began in earnest. I pulled harder and harder, until the great spiraling thing was unseated and eventually separated from the trunk of my tree. The victory was potent but small. I knew there was more to my final enemy--miles for all I knew.

The roots below the mother were incredible. A new network, vastly more complex and interwoven than the separate systems I had found beneath the sprouts. Those had been mere scribblings, but this was a masterpiece. And so I raged and pulled and dug until my fingers bled.

By the time I looked up, the sky was red.

Dusk was my first guess, but my phone told me otherwise. Breath raked the insides of my throat as I stood--desperate to make sense of the time. 5:13 am. The numbers were right there at the top of my lock screen. Of course this was impossible. For that to be true, it would mean I had been outside not only all afternoon, but all night. Noticing neither the changes in light or temperature or anything else beyond the battle.

But there it was.

Absently, I looked at the ground. Before me, bathed in the red light of dawn was my hated enemy. The Mother Root was dead. Her full form exhumed and strewn out for all to see. Catharsis coursed as I reached and took up the body of my defeated foe--lifting it like a fisherman displaying the catch of his life. Holding her like that, she looked like a bolt copper lightning frozen in mid-strike.

By God, I had won. I was exhausted and covered in layers of grime and who knew how many fresh wounds, but it had all been worth it. I hadn't mowed the lawn and I probably couldn't build a retaining wall if my life depended on it, but in that moment, I most definitely *had triumphant.*

Nine days have passed.

Night time has become something to dread.

A time ruled by fitful, troubled visions. The dream-scenarios change from night to night, though there is only one ending. Eventually, something will be uncovered or pushed aside--a blanket, a rug, maybe a pile of unfolded laundry. Every time it is the same.

The vines are there. Always. Haunting me. Growing just beneath.

I didn't go to work last week. My wife, my daughters, they don't understand. Can't understand. They weren't there. They didn't rip a million miles of red root from the earth with their bare hands, only to find more and more *and more.* Because just when you think the end is near, all you've really found is another fork in the road. Cut off one head and two more grow in its place. No, that's something else. The hydra has heads. Me on the other hand, all I have is the Goddamned bittersweet. And bittersweet has roots. Of course, now I know the truth. They weren't just roots.

Every one of them was *her.*

I can remember tenth grade biology. Learning about the systems of the human body. At the time, it was the nervous system that struck me most. When I close my eyes, I can still see the illustrations in the textbook. The veins and arteries with their uncountable branching pathways. How they looked like bolts of red lighting.

Most of my cuts are healed now. The one behind my shoulder leaks, but since my wife took the girls to stay at her aunt's house, I stopped dressing it. Without her here to make a fuss, I just didn't see the point.

I noticed the lines the day before yesterday.

In the mirror, I could see them radiating from the oozing spot behind my shoulder. They look like rivers. Dark, ominous, things flowing down my arm-- across my chest. There is no pain, but my limbs move with a tightness that wasn't there before. In the slightest gesture, I can feel her--the mother root.

I don't know the how, only the what. She's inside me. Growing. Changing.

Terraforming.

Every day, every hour she grows a little more. Reaches a little farther. Past organs, through meat, coiling around bone. I can't say how much longer I have.

All I know is, I have to get her out.

THE ROOT OF ALL NITE

The Root of All Noise

For Marcus Wade, exploring nature had always been one of his *things*. A hobby that served as a way of working both exercise and a bit of adventure into an otherwise banal routine. For him, it was a kind of scheduled solitude. A chance to get away from the bump and the grind.

Away from the noise.

Wade had learned the labyrinth. Memorized all of the intersecting trails and where they led. Some days he would allow himself to get lost and meander for hours--going from loop to loop until the sunlight began to wane. Other times he would follow the Thunderbolt all the way to the Appalachian Trail and then proceed the remaining half mile to the summit of Mount Greylock. He couldn't have guessed how many times he had seen that tall granite memorial, nor how many sandwiches had been consumed in its presence. He would gaze up, musing on what a pain in the ass it must have been to haul all that rock to such a remote location or how much it looked like a titanic chess piece.

Really, it was shit like that that reinforced his decision to keep hiking a solo affair. In Wade's experience, company kept his mind on everything he was trying to escape. Work or traffic or whatever bullshit show just hit whatever bullshit streaming service. It was static, all of it.

Just more Goddamned noise.

* * *

Wade's ears prickled at the sound of sudden voices.

There were hikers maybe an eighth of a mile back. They were moving faster than he was and would catch up soon. The question was, whether or not they would keep that pace or slow down and try to make friends. All Wade knew for certain was that very soon, he was going to have company.

This was his first hike in a very long time and he damn sure wasn't ready for his solitude to end. Turning, he gazed up the hill to his left and into the dense forest that surrounded the clearly marked walking trail.

Well, shit. Wade considered the path untravelled. *Do you want a fresh start or not?*

When the hikers passed below, they did not see Marcus Wade. For he had disobeyed the written warnings. Had abandoned the path and scrambled up nearly fifteen feet of embankment. Out of breath but blissfully unseen, he watched as a group of loud twenty-somethings passed by. His heart pounded in his chest. Standing in the shadow of a tall tree, Wade's hand slid down to a stomach he had not been proud of in almost a decade. But such thoughts were useless. Shame was just more bullshit. Just noise.

For the better part of an hour, the going was difficult. Saying to hell with something always felt great in the moment, but the follow through was a pain in the ass. Now Wade was facing the full brunt of not just being older, but away from the game for so damn long. How had he gotten so soft? Despite being rhetorical, the question managed to dust off a potential answer. A face he did not want to think about.

Laurie. Even now, the thought of her made his blood boil.

She was the real reason why he was here. Why Wade was currently hiking up a treacherous slope like some jackass kid half his age. Sure--whatever he was trying to prove was to himself, but she was the reason.

Leaning against a massive trunk, Wade tried to focus only on his breathing. On the steady kick drum beat, pounding in his chest. For almost a full minute he stood like that until thirst crept up his throat. The vision of a water bottle appeared in his mind--all new and red and made of special space age technology. Wade twisted to remove his pack, suddenly desperate to get at the water which he knew would still be perfectly ice cold and just the thing he needed.

That was when his left foot shot out behind him.

Wade's eyes went wide as his vision blurred. He saw the ground rushing up and a flash of light and pain when it hit. His hands grasped at the ground but uselessly. The speed he picked up was impressive but by some miracle, the man's body never entered a tumble. Instead he continued to slide backwards as rocks and sticks raked the tender flesh of his belly.

The impact came, as most do, quite suddenly.

When consciousness returned, Wade's first thought was that his right arm was asleep. Worse, the hand was still full of painful pins and needles and hadn't yet reached the fully numb, phantom limb stage. He blinked, swore and realized the taste in his mouth was blood.

Looking up, he could see what had stopped him from sliding the remaining half mile down the slope. One strap of his backpack had caught on something which was sticking out of the ground. Something which just as easily could have caught him in the eye or shoulder instead. Carefully, he reached out with the hand that wasn't numb--gripping onto the object that had saved him. The thing he first assumed was a twisted old root.

Fingers reached, clenched and the root did the rest.

Wade's head was raised six feet into the air and it swam the whole way-- phasing through flashes of light and synapse that quickly morphed into familiar shapes. The image was a woman's face. A woman he loved. A woman he hated. Laurie's face was as beautiful as ever. In fact, her perfect smokey eyes looked even sexier this way. Enhanced somehow by the spattering of fresh blood.

Gasping in horror, Wade released the root--instinctively pressing the hand to his forehead. Consciousness, it turned out, had returned with one hell of a headache. Wincing to the point of tears, he spat and coughed before hauling himself back to his feet. Using a nearby trunk for stability, Wade remembered his phone. One hand plunged into his pocket but was pulled back immediately.

"*Shit!!*" He sucked air in through his teeth, staring in disbelief at the translucent, needle-thin sliver protruding from the tip of his ring finger. While Wade's stomach turned, his good hand shakily pulled out the glass and flicked it away. The phone had been thoroughly smashed. Only by carefully turning the pocket inside-out did his fingers avoid further damage.

"Of course." He frowned, angrily throwing the broken thing.

Wade squinted down at the old root that had saved him. Watched as red saliva dripped down--sliding beneath the leaves and the earth. He looked at his still bloody fingertips and had the strangest urge to touch them to the twisted thing. To give it just a little more. Immediately revolted by the idea, Wade proceded to clean and bandage the cuts using various supplies from his pack.

That's it? He thought, shaking his head at the root. *That little thing stopped your two hundred and forty pound ass?*

Head still throbbing, Wade frowned. God, it felt like a grapefruit had taken up residence in his skull. Touching his temple made him feel instantly light headed. For a moment, all thoughts were replaced by a distant sound. Something like static.

Wiping away tears on a dirty sleeve, Wade looked over to his miracle pack. One strap was still looped around the root-thing as if in some mockery of ring toss. As he stared, Wade's eyes shifted again. This time to the slope above. The track he had made on the way down was a crude Slip 'N Slide of exposed mud that ran, for the most part, in a straight line. The weird thing was the last ten feet or so. That's when the track took an abrupt turn, leading directly to a thing that was looking less and less like a root.

The twisted thing was about eight inches long. Its surface was a uniform black but it did not appear to be made of wood. Starting at the end, Wade could see it was covered with a series of concentric lines--each circling the object, one after another. The comparison which entered his mind was growth rings. Not of a tree but the kind seen in the spiraling horns of antelopes or even bighorn sheep.

Wade reached for his pack with care. He did not want to touch the strange object in the ground. Not again. The pack was lifted slowly to insure the edges of the strap never touched. It felt a little like a game. As if he were playing some inverted version of Operation.

"Remove your pieces... collect the fee," he said in a drone. "Just don't touch the fucking sides..."

Wade hadn't thought about that stupid commercial in years. He snickered but there was no humor in it.

"Goddamn you, Laurie."

The setting was a dusty antique shop with a clever name he couldn't recall--some stupid play on words. His ex had always been a sucker for that kind of stuff. Though Wade spent his time looking through boxes of old comics, Laurie did her usual full inspection of absolutely every single item in the Goddamned store.

"Wade!" She half whispered-half shouted. Running, holding a flat box in her hands. "Wade!"

At the sound of his name, Wade peeled himself away from an old issue of Battlemania and the question on the cover which asked: 'Who can stop the Undertaker?". With a raised eyebrow, he focused on the thing in Laurie's hands. This flat, rectangular object which was being presented with a degree of reverence usually reserved for ancient holy relics, or maybe a pizza.

"I can't believe it! It's a freaking original!" She blurted out. "A vintage 1965, just like the one Nan kept at her cottage in Maine!"

In that moment, Wade felt all the color drain from his face. He couldn't believe it. After all this time, she actually found a copy of that stupid, piece of crap game.

"It's complete in box?" Wade tried to keep all emotion from his voice. "How much?"

"$120," Laurie grinned in that way she had. A look so sexy it could convince wallpaper to strip. "I mean, the metal edges are rusty, but the surface decal is in pretty good shape!"

"One twenty? Are they on crack? You know those things go for like forty bucks on eBay."

Laurie's mouth turned up into a smirk. "Screw eBay. It's all about the thrill of the hunt and you know it."

The bitch of it was, Wade did know. And though it pained him to do so, he put down the issue of Battlemania. With a sigh, he began filing all the comics he had put aside back into their dusty long-boxes. "That is a hell of a markup, Lor." He grumbled.

"Oh come on, babe. You know I've been looking for this like, *forever*. Besides, I'll pay you back tonight." Laurie flashed another grin--making sure to press one of her primary curves against her boyfriend's leg on her way to the register.

"Damn it, Wade." As usual, the phrase was too low for anyone to hear. It had become something of a secret call sign. An audible cue that a tiny bit more of the man's soul had just leaked out. First the solo running treks and then by degrees, more and more of himself. Lost.

Past You Buy

That was it. The stupid name of the stupid shop. If only the sign had read Uncle Al's Dusty Old Shit or something, Laurie might never have looked twice.

Secretly, Wade had always hated that Goddamned game. He'd owned it as a kid--gotten it as a gift for his eighth birthday. Aside from a few packs of wrestling cards, it had been the only present his mom had given him that year. She had proclaimed that the game was a classic, but she was wrong?

As far as Wade was concerned, Operation wasn't a classic anything beyond a classic assault on the eyes and ears! Hell, just playing it made his blood pressure go up. Plus there was the game's alleged patient or victim, as young Wade saw it, since the poor bastard was awake the whole time. Cavity Sam was horrifying. Stark naked and devoid of genitals, the cartoon man's eyes and mouth were aghast as he beheld the horrors being done to him. Worst of all, where his nose should be, a huge red light bulb had been surgically grafted.

No doubt about it, Operation sucked. And of course, of all the girls in all the coffee shops in the all world, she had to walk into his. Laurie Bettis--the girl obsessed with finding a vintage copy of his most hated childhood possession.

For years Wade had tried to rise above. Refusing to let on about his hatred for the game and even perusing an online auction or two. But when push came to shove, hitting that BUY NOW button was too hard. Doing so would have been like ordering a burger made from quinoa or purchasing a shirt with Ben

Shapiro on the front. For Marcus Wade, it was something he couldn't bring himself to do in a million years. Because, in the end, he still remembered what it felt like to feel helpless. To wake up in the middle of the night, too scared to breathe.

Oh sure, some kids were haunted by clowns or mummies or drug dealers, but for Wade, the boogey man was called Cavity fucking Sam. It was why, for almost two years, he slept with a blanket over his head--afraid that if he looked, he might see a pale man there. A man wearing nothing but a horrific grimace--his body riddled in bloodless holes. A man stepping slowly from the shadows of a doorway, bathed in the soft red light of his own fucking nose.

Even now, Wade could hear it. The shrill, brain-splitting buzz that shot through his fillings and out the top of his head.

Wade looked down to the root that wasn't. He stared, wondering just how it could have hooked the arm strap in the first place. The angle, the amount that was sticking out of the ground... none of it made sense. He could have been impaled--or, in a more ideal scenario, just bumped into it and kept going. And that is exactly what he resolved to do. To leave the mysteries alone and to be happy that aside from a few bumps and bruises, he hadn't suffered any real damage.

After pulling out his water bottle, he indulged in a long, well-earned drink. Allowing himself to be healing by the relief and the healing coldness of the water.

"Not even five?" Wade raised an eyebrow at his watch, then shrugged. "I guess there's still time. Question is... which way you gonna point your ass, old man?"

Wade looked down the slope. Through the trees he could see light. He knew the tried and true Thunderbolt trail was still down there. Still waiting for his return, just as it had for the past twelve years. Part of him wanted to drop on the ground right then, To crab-walk like the old man he was, all the way down the embankment and into that light. Then he could follow the Thunderbolt to the Appalachian, eat his bologna on wheat, flip off the monument and drive home--or possibly to the hospital.

Yes. Part of him wanted to do all of that... but the rest of him said fuck it.

Some time later, after more running than he had done in years, Wade came to a stop. Nearly breathless he bent over, bracing both hands on his knees. Right then he was thankful no one could see him.

"God damn," Wade spat between gulps of air--hands fumbling with the zipper of his pack.

There was plenty of water left in the space-age bottle, but Wade allowed himself only a small mouthful before returning the bottle to his pack. It was one of his rules from way back. Always save the last sip for the car and you never go thirsty. But his mind wasn't on his thirst, nor on the heartbeat that felt strong enough to punch through his sternum. Right then, Wade was more interested on a small white arrow.

He had drawn it on the tree almost two hours earlier--right where the embankment had finally flattened out. Though he never got lost, Wade always brought an industrial paint pen on his solo hikes. Just in case. Sure you weren't supposed to do this kind of thing, but who would know? Only an idiot would wander this far from the trail.

Wade looked at the arrow and at the direction it was indicating. He knew exactly what he would find if he followed the slope down in that direction. In some ways, he could even feel it.

"Damn it, Wade. Just leave it alone." Saying this, he could feel the distant pulses of a once bad headache. "There's got to be a safer way down. At home, you can use the landline to call..."

"*Who?*" Spoke a noise like liquid static. A voice that swarmed and buzzed and that Marcus Wade took for his own thoughts. "*Call who, Wade? Not her. Not after what she said. After what you did.*"

After a dozen years as a couple, Mark and Laurie Wade had honed arguing to an artform but that last one had been something worse. The rage, the pettiness--all of it had been real next level stuff. As had the truths that had slipped out. Especially that big one at the end. The thing about why she was always home so late after those Thursday night shifts.

"Dave?" Wade spat out the name as if it were venom drawn from a wound.

"Who the fuck is *Dave*?"

"One of the other bartenders--Jesus, you're so wrapped up in your own shit, sometimes I think you can't even hear me anymore. *Dave.* He usually works days because he goes to night school. Thursdays is our only shift together and..." Laurie's voice hitched for a second. "I never planned any of it, okay? I didn't. It just *happened.* And then, I don't know... it *kept* happening."

Wade's heart was pounding--his throat dry. The memories of that last fight buzzed like a swarm of horny botflies and Wade attempted to shoo them away as such. Then, with some well placed confusion, he looked down at his hand. The fingers were wrapped around something spiraled and dark--something like a root. Though he had no memory of climbing back down the hill, Wade was gripping the root-thing so aggressively, his knuckles were white. He watched as an outside observer would, as a small drop of blood beaded at the edge of the bandaged fingertip. When the small drop of red touched the root, the root drank it in.

"How...?" Wade could feel his creeping rage. "How long?"

"Does it matter?"

"Damn it, Lor! *How fucking long*?"

He could remember spitting out the question. The demand for an insignificant shred of information that would change nothing. Help nothing. Laurie's answer had come out wet and blubbery but also full of anger. That might have been what had bothered Wade the most. In that moment, in spite of everything she had done... *Laurie* was pissed at *him.*

Unwilling to hear more, the eyes of Marcus Wade had searched for escape. He needed to get away from the fight and from his new truth. That he was married to a woman who had cheated on him. Nine years of dating and three as husband and wife and she was cheating on him with fucking Dave the daytime bartender.

Wade had looked to the door, then the shelf that proudly displayed a vintage copy of his least favorite game. The same game he'd bought her on that day in the antique shop with the stupid name. Car keys. Where the fuck were his car keys? He turned to the key holder, but his peg was empty. Fort the third time, he padded his pockets--confirming their emptiness. That was when he remembered. When he got home he had put them down next to the microwave. And there they were still. Connected to his the fob from a local garage that only needed two more punches before he could get a free oil change.

Without a word, Wade slammed a hand down on the counter and lifted what was there. That was when Laurie's expression had changed. Becoming something that Wade had never seen her wear before. Her eyes--red and full of tears became open windows of pure white horror.

"What are you doing? Put that down." Now she was giving the demands. "*Damn* it, Wade--I said put that fucking thing down right now!"

Wade had been confused then and was confused now. In his mind, the long kitchen knife didn't make sense.

What happened next was a blur. Pure emotion and impulse, but mostly noise.

His hands had begun to work by themselves. As they were thrust into the moist black earth, a wave of relief and ecstasy washed over Marcus Wade. He worked in a frenzy, as more of the dark soil and leaves were removed from around the strange root-like object in the ground. And with every thrust, his body was racked with a flash of pure distilled purpose. Whatever the thing he was exhuming was, it wanted the same thing that Wade had wanted that night in the kitchen.

"*Escape*".

Wade's body was in overdrive. Sweat cascaded down the sides of his face and into his eyes--stinging them. He should have been tired. Should have passed out from the exhaustion of being wiped from his first good hike in almost twelve years. His nose was bleeding but that didn't matter. He never thought about the sharp taste in his mouth or the fact that his heart was probably less than ten beats away from a full-on attack.

"*She looked good that night,*" Spoke the liquid static in his brain. "*Better when you were finished. Those big smokey eyes really made the red pop.*"

"Stop it!" Shouted Wade, continuing to toss handfuls of earth behind him.

"Oh, what's the matter? I know you remember how good it felt. How deliciously fucking righteous."

"I said..." Wade's hands become fists. "Stop it!"

He dropped to the ground, clutching both ears, cringing in agony. The buzzing noise was so loud, he could barely think. He tried to remember back to that night in the kitchen. Tried to think how in God's name he could have done those horrible things. It felt impossible--unthinkable. And yet he could see himself lifting the knife. Could feel the smile on his face and the orgasmic ecstasy of Laurie's blood as it flowed out of her in a great red gush.

"Jesus Christ." He hissed through clenched teeth. "I really did that, didn't I? Lor? Oh God, I didn't mean to... I didn't..."

"Oh, Wade," Said the noise. *"You never planned for any of it. It just sort of... happened. Isn't that right? It was only an accident. A happy righteous little accident. Just like all those others times."*

"What other times? No! There were no other times!"

As he shouted, flecks of blood shot from Wade's lips and hit the exposed object. There was almost three feet of it visible now and the further down it went the thicker it became.

"Tell that to the man in the shop with the clever name... what was it called again?"

The name Past You Buy slithered through Wade's brain.

"That's the one," The buzzing static cooed, sounding much too pleased with itself. *"The cost of that game you purchased was exorbitant. Price gouging of the highest order. You asked the man to come down to $75 but he could see how much the prize meant to her. He knew he didn't have to lose a single dollar on the deal and so... he didn't. But later that night, you went back."*

"No."

"YES! You planned on giving the man a piece of your mind but things played out differently, didn't they?"

"No they didn't. I never went back there!"

"Oh yes you did, Wade. You went back to do a little gouging of your own."

Wade let out a sob. The noise in his head was making pictures. Not as clear as the ones of Laurie and the kitchen had been, but he could make them out. Could see his knife slide directly into the shopkeeper's left eye. Not dead center, but near the tear duct. With a sudden rush of disgust, Wade could hear the scraping sound of metal on bone as the knife turned. Could feel a kind of pleasant release as the eye finally popped out of its socket, coming to rest on the man's cheek.

"STOP!!"

And just like that the noise did stop. Wade was on his side, sobbing uncontrollably into the hill.

"That..." Wade's voice was weak--insignificant. "That didn't happen! I didn't do any of it. Not to that asshole in the shop... and not to her. I fucking *love* Laurie. I could never, *never* hurt her. These memories aren't real. I didn't lift a knife off that counter, just my fucking car keys! Sure, I was pissed--and yeah, right then, all I wanted was for her to hurt as bad as I was... but the only thing I stabbed was that fucking game! Over and over with my key and it felt great! She cried, called me a psycho, and then she left. That is what happened."

"Who are you trying to convince here, Wade? I mean, you were there. I'm just some voice in a hill."

Wade opened his eyes just as dawn was creeping across the sky. He was confused and scared and in a considerable amount of pain.

He looked over at the horn. That was the only word for it now. Something like the spiraling cranial appendage of an African antelope, but titanic and black. True black. The color of malice. The original eight inches still stood above ground level, but now a massive crater encircled the object. Around four feet across and deep. *Really* deep.

Wade tried to say something, but his throat was too dry for that. Remembering his water bottle and the last sip inside, he looked around for his pack. God, what happened? Did he really sleep here last night? Just exposed like this on the side of a hill he wasn't even supposed to be on?

After getting to his feet, Wade stumbled over to where his pack was lying. His fingers felt stiff and useless so he used his teeth to work the zipper. With one great jerk of his head, the bag was opened and the water bottle removed.

Still cold. Wade thought. Then he coughed, sputtered and closed his eyes. Only after catching his breath, did he look down at his fingers. They were hideous. Caked with black soil and blood. One was even missing the entire nail. He moved closer to the edge of the massive crater and stealthily peered down. It looked like a circular grave with a great spiraling monolith raised in the center.

"Such sweet sacrifice," Purred the noise. *"Nine hours of labor and two of rest. Your blood and passion have rejuvenated me, Wade. Granted me strength enough."*

The buzzing static was deeper now--rattling the nerves behind the man's eyes. Though it was almost impossible to concentrate on anything else, Wade forced out a question.

"Strength enough for what?"

"For what we discussed."

Suddenly, the side of the hill began to heave. As the pitch of the ground increased, Wade was sent tumbling and rolling. By some miracle, he managed to loop his arm around a tree. Lying on his stomach, the man looked up in horror as the hill undulated--swelling in great waves like the ocean. It was as if he were witnessing the birth of a new volcano... or maybe something a hell of a lot worse.

"Remember what we discussed!" The liquid static sounded excited but it felt like an ice pick in the ear. *"Remember our bargain!"*

Right then, Wade couldn't remember making a bargain. Then again, it was all he could to to hang on.

"Only thing I remember is you Total-Recalling a bunch of lies into my brain!" He bellowed at the top of his lungs. Shouting with every last ounce of strength he had. "I didn't do any of that shit and I didn't make any deal with the devil!"

"On that we agree." The noise sounded bemused. *"The devil is only a story. I am older than such things."*

When the ground shook again, trees started sticking out at wrong angles. That was when Wade let go. With no other choice, he allowed himself to slide down and down--landing at last, in a heap on the Thunderbolt trail. He got to his feet just in time to see a great section of the embankment crumble away, forming a cave-like hollow. And from the darkness of that newly formed cave, something moved.

"The memories I presented were not lies, Wade. They were possibilities. Laurie, the shop man, that bitch who cut you in line at the Post Office, they all deserve to pay. I have seen your heart, Marcus Wade. I know your true enemy. The totem of your childhood torment. He who stole your dreams. Your... innocence. Oh yes, I've seen the naked man with the red nose."

"What?" Wade couldn't believe what he was hearing. "You mean the fucking Operation guy?! But he... he's not real!"

"No, Wade. But the man who hurt you is. Remember him now. Remember his name."

Wade's heart was racing. He couldn't move, couldn't even breathe. Muscles were frozen in place as the noise increased in both volume and intensity. Filling every secret place as he stared into the perfect dark of that newly formed cave--trying his damndest not to vomit.

"Lewis." The name slithered from the recesses of Wade's brain, trembling past his lips, numbing them. "Lewis Carmody. Oh my God."

The pain was too unexpected, too great. For almost a full minute Marcus Wade said nothing.

"Mom," He began slowly. "She worked nights then. Usually, a girl two blocks down would watch me, but one time she couldn't. I don't think Mom and Lewis had dated for very long but she didn't have a choice. Didn't have anyone else to ask. Lewis fucking Carmody. Yeah... I remember he drank a lot. And I remember his nose. It was big. And it was red. Oh God. Oh my fucking God."

Wade clapped both hands over his mouth. No longer concerned with the oppressive noise which had focused into a tone. A laser beam of pure sound bisecting his brain.

"God is not here, Wade. Only us. Only possibility."

Wade was sobbing into his hands. Glaring at the shifting darkness of the newly formed cave as three lids retracted to reveal a wet, glassy surface. It was an eye the size of a truck tire. A horrible thing, covered in veins, wreathed in dirt and boils--as brown as the earth, with an oblong pupil. Just beholding it caused something to snap inside the man called Marcus Wade.

The hillside rumbled and quaked and finally heaved with the force of buried dynamite. The forgotten thing which had slumbered since the world was young shrugged off its cloak of earth. It had too many eyes, too many nostrils, all on a goat-like head that supported a pair of towering horns, long enough to gouge the sky. Without warning, the buried God lunged forward, slamming a pair of enormous cloven hands on either side of the tiny little man.

Unable to do much else, Wade began to laugh. The noise had filled him up. It buzzed in his throat, behind his brain and in the ragged, bloody tips of his fingers.

MONSTER
FINANCING
AVAILABLE

Monster Financing Available

The sedan was black, maybe ten years old. In dramatic fashion, both front doors flew open--gaping for a second or two like the gill flaps of some monstrous fish.

It was the passenger who stepped out first. Mrs. Nale wore a black suit with matching bindi and a rather hooked nose. Her hair was long but pulled back in a military-style bun that made her look ready to mount a corporate takeover. As she squinted into the dusty haze of the Missouri afternoon, the woman did not look pleased.

From the driver's side, stepped a very large, very well dressed man. Mr. Boothe rose slowly to his full height before adjusting the lapel on his jacket. Though technically one quarter German, the man's Apache ancestry was all anyone saw. His stern face was mired in harsh lines and, like his cohort, the man was all business.

The pair had driven far and spoken only when necessary, as was their custom. This after all, was hardly their first rodeo. Both doors to the black sedan were slammed in unison.

Mr. Boothe twisted a shoulder around, producing a series of pops in his spine.   Then he stepped forward--an act which resulted in an unexpected *crunch*. Raising an eyebrow, he bent to pick up the small rectangular container.

The two compartments were empty but for traces of dirty orange sludge.

"What is *that*?" Asked Mrs. Nale in a perfunctory tone. Her accent, vaguely English.

"It's... you know those crackers that come with the little compartment full of cheese?" Mr. Boothe presented the item for his partner's benefit, quickly noting her continued lack of comprehension. "They come with a little red stick so you can spread the cheese, but most just use it like a shovel."

"American cuisine at its finest, I'm sure." The woman turned, sliding on dark glasses which matched the pair worn by her partner.

Holding the bit of refuse with the fewest fingers possible, Mr. Boothe sighed. "There better be a trashcan up ahead."

The agents moved down a street that looked as if it hadn't been repaved in a century. West Pleasant road was lined with a combination of parked cars, half-naked trees, sun-fried fields and the husks of old buildings. The tragic story of the town was one these travelling customer service agents knew well. After all, the heart of every coal town is its mine. Once that stops beating, some folks have the sense to move on. Most, however, simply rot on the vine.

As Boothe and Nale weighed what they could see of the location, it made an elegant kind of sense. Red Ridge, Missouri was exactly the kind of run-down speck of used-to-be-something, the company sought out. Passing an old Chevy Vega, Mr. Boothe took note of a sticker on the rear bumper. Bold white letters set in a green field.

"Rock out with your croc-trout?" The man read the phrase as if it were a question."

"I... don't understand." Mrs. Nale sounded just barely intrigued. "Is that some pop culture reference I'm not getting?"

"Hmm," The man grunted, shook his head. "More like a spin on an already bad joke. Crass, but creative. My bet was on *Red Ridge Monster.*"

The woman turned her head, offering no emotion. "Your bet is always the name of the town *plus* monster."

"That's because I play the odds. Look." Boothe indicated ahead, to an old wooden sign which proclaimed: WEST PLEASANT BEACH. NO LIFEGUARD ON DUTY.

As they soon discovered, the sign marked the entrance to a dirt lot which was full of cars. As the agents crossed the parking area, many more bumper stickers could be seen. Some even had drawings of the creature itself. Missouri's brand new local legend was depicted as a four legged dinosaur with a shark fin on the back.

Mr. Boothe turned to look directly at his partner. "I thought the specimen was a fish."

"That's because you didn't actually *read the report.*" Nale sighed sharply. "The lab listed *huso huso, hydrocynus goliath, arapaima arapaima,* and *crocodylus johnstoni.* But you know how the process works. There's always a bit of this or that used to fill gaps in the sequencing. Likely, the lab made this Red Ridge specimen more *croc* than trout."

"Hmm." Grunted Mr. Boothe. "That *does* sound like them."

Approaching an old metal drum labeled TRASH, he released the crumpled cheese and cracker container in his hand, then pushed three large fingers into a front pocket. Along with the intended packet of disinfectant wipes, a small white rectangle was extracted. Mr. Boothe never noticed this however. Never saw the object tumble in the air and dance lazily to the ground. He was much too focused on cleaning the areas between every one of his fingers.

Before long, the sounds of a rumpus crowd reached the ears of Mr. Boothe and Mrs. Nale. Just past the lot was a sprawling green park that spilled into the lake itself. Local thrill seekers were all around--all hoping to catch a glimpse of the lake's newest resident. Folks were gathered around picnic tables or sprawled on towels, while little ones ran and played. But none of them mattered.

"I see him. That's definitely our contact." Mrs. Nale said, pointing with an annoyed smirk. "His photograph was in the report. Walton J. Bowater--town administrator of this little *slice of heaven.*"

Mr. Boothe turned to see a fat, balding, politician-type who seemed to stand out from the crowd like a beacon. Though he waved and smiled at the people moving past, his body language was tight. Both relieved and anxious at the same time.

"Bowater, huh?" Boothe rolled the name over his tongue. "Guy looks like he's staring down an oncoming bus."

"Well, what did you expect?" Tittered Mrs. Nale under her breath. "The man's a politician."

As they approached, the company's newest disgruntled customer was in full blanch at the pair of dark skinned, darker suited government-spook-types walking his way.

"Jesus. Are you *them*?" Bowater asked in a quieted voice. "What am I saying--of course you are. Look at you!" He smiled broadly and waved to a passing family. "Alright, so what do I call you?"

The fat man spoke in a heavy drawl. His eyes continuing to shift between the man and the woman. Producing a handkerchief, he dabbed the sweat from his hairless pate before stuffing it back away.

"Names are irrelevant." Said the female agent. "All that matters is that we are from the company and that we are here."

Bowater turned to look the woman in the face, but his eyes didn't stop there. She was a foot shorter than the Indian guy--light on curves but sort of sexy in a bitch-on-wheels kinda way.

"Jesus fly-fishin' Christ, you two look like the Goddamned Men in Black. Couldn't you have dressed a little--I don't know, *inconspicuous?*" Bowater slapped his own forehead. "Aw hell--not like you'd be able to blend in anyhow. Not in *this* town. So... which is it? *Dot or feather?* In these progressive times, you hate to say the wrong thing--but shit, I can never tell."

Looking down at that sweaty politician's face made the jaws of Mr. Boothe clench. In that moment, he had a need to say or possibly do something very unprofessional. Fortunately, the touch of a small hand on his arm, stilled him. Tactile interaction tended to be a last resort with Mrs. Nale, but it produced the desired effect.

"Mr. Bowater." The woman's voice was calm, free of offense. She even smiled a tight smile. "Now that we are here, perhaps you can take us somewhere more *private* to discuss your *more pressing* concerns?"

"Concerns?!" Bowater scoffed, sending spittle into the air. "That's one way of putting what I got." Adopting a smile which gleefully parodied courtesy, the town administrator threw an arm out in a flourish. "Why don't y'all just step inside my office."

The two agents exchanged an expressionless glance before acquiescing.

As the three crossed the bustling beach, they passed a vendor table where a shirtless boy of about fifteen was purchasing something. After handing the cash to the vendor, the kid grinned at the design of his new shirt before slipping it on.

"*Rock out with your croc-trout!*" He exclaimed, clearly pleased with his purchase. "Awesome!"

Mr. Boothe took note of the slogan written there. Immediately realizing that the vendor man's inventory must also include bumper stickers.

"*Hats, t-shirts, water bottles! Whatever you need, I got it.*" Shouted the stringy-haired vendor man, just as another group jogged his way. "*Get your official croc-trout merchandise right here!*"

Mrs. Nale said nothing but rolled her eyes about as hard as they would go.

The beach ended at the start of a trail leading into a section of woods that continued around the rest of the lake. This was roped off, marked by another sign that read: TRAIL CLOSED BY ORDER OF GAME WARDEN. Ignoring the warning, Bowater stepped over the rope but held it up for the woman. Ignoring the gesture, Mrs. Nale proceeded to walk around the post.

"Your Game Warden is Thomas Dowdy, yes?" She said, not really asking. "We are going to need to speak with him as soon as possible."

Bowater didn't answer. Instead he once again dabbed his head and slipped farther down the path. By the time all three were fully in the woods, the fat man dropped all remaining pretenses.

"The thing is, darlin'... Tom Dowdy never made it home last night. He's well... *missing.*"

Mr. Boothe exchanged another glance with his partner. "When did you last speak to him?"

"Oh good, the big one speaks!" Bowater's unbridled anxiety was about as subtle as rhinestone cufflinks. "Shit, I don't know. Last night, around six?"

"Are you asking or telling?" Boothe did not sound amused.

"Uh... telling, I think. Yeah, had to be around then because calling Tom was the last thing I did before leaving the office. I needed him to swing by on his way home. To... hang that damn sign back there."

Again, the agents looked warily at one another.

"God. I must have had two dozen calls from his wife this morning. Poor

Sheila was a wreck. Kept saying the same thing over and over. How Tom had *never* not come home before. And with what happened last week--with those damn kids... well, let's just say I had a feeling Tom hadn't finally run off with Wilma Blanchard." The fat man looked miserable. "Anyway, once I'd calmed Shiela down, I came here and noticed *that*." He pointed. "Believe you me, whatever in God's name *that* is, it's new."

Ahead was a muddy embankment leading straight down to the water. The mud looked strange there--sporting a series of strange parallel grooves. Looking more serious than ever, Boothe crossed the distance, then knelt down to extend a hand. Those long fingers came close to the earth, seeming to hover there.

"What are we looking at, Mr. Boothe?" The voice of Mrs. Nail was clinical.

"It's definitely a slide." The Apache's voice was low and grim. "I'd say the specimen exited and re-entered the lake right here. In that order. Twelve hours ago, maybe less." His eyes shot from place to place, all around and further down the embankment. "Crocodiles make these when they sun themselves up on the shore. After a few hours, when the body temperature is just right, the animal will just slide back in the water. But these marks here..." he swung a hand over different patch of mud that was less smooth than the first. "These tells a different story. There was a struggle here."

Mrs. Nale kneeled down for a closer inspection. "Have you seen anything like this before?"

"Sure." Said Mr. Boothe. "In Africa. Along the Nile. After a crocodile hits a zebra and drags it under."

"Well, there are no zebras in Missouri, Mr. Boothe." Said Walton J. Bowater from right where he was. "What we did have was a hell of a fish and game warden by the name of Tom Dowdy. And those kids last week... Matt Chance and the McFaye girl, Roberta--*Bobby*. God damn it. I've known those kids since they were born." Bowater had started to ring his pudgy hands. He did not look well. "Shit, they weren't half done with high school."

Mr. Boothe nodded. "The installation date was March fourth, yeah?"

"Correct." Nodded the woman, checking her wrist for the time. "Almost three months before the first casualty. That was five days ago, on the twenty-second. Mr. Bowater... you mentioned that Thomas Dowdy was likely taken last night. Do you know if the first two victims were taken around the same time of day?"

The fat politician dabbed his forehead, then stepped closer to what the tall man had called a slide.

"Please." She continued. "If we can determine a feeding pattern, removal of the specimen will go more smoothly."

"You keep saying that. The *specimen.*" Bowater's eyes were glassy with guilt and with fear. "I think you mean your Goddamned *monster,* ain't that right? Our brand new, custom-built local legend--so amazing it was guaranteed to put Red Ridge, Missouri back on the map?" Bowater was speaking loudly, with large sweeps of his arms. "And here we are, three months in and what have we got to show for it? A few lousy t-shirts? Some bumper stickers? Sure Sadie's is booked to the end of the month for the first time since she can remember, but *three deaths?!* This is *not* what we signed up for! Not what we *paid* for with the hard-earned tax dollars of this here community. No ma'am."

After a few seconds, Mrs. Nale cleared her throat in the manner of an interrupting librarian. A tight little *hm-hm.* "The term is *paying,* Mr. Bowater. Not paid."

The fat man turned toward the agent woman. His expression, one of consternation. "Excuse me?"

"You said *paid for...* but that is simply not accurate." Mrs. Nale spoke in an overtly soothing fashion. "The company would, first and foremost, like to express our sincerest regrets for any suffering you and your town have experienced. But this does not alter the fact that nothing has been paid for. At least, not in full." Mrs. Nale smiled tightly, thinly. "If you would be so kind to remember, Mr. Bowater... you selected the *financing option.*"

Bowater licked the sweat from his lips and just stared back, utterly dumbstruck.

"My point, of course, is that even after my partner and I have finished with the removal, payment for the specimen will continue for the period as previously set by the aforementioned contract. If at any time it is determined that your town is in breach of our agreement, well... let's just say you *won't* be seeing us in court." Mrs. Nale removed a long silver spike from her hair to let it gleam in the light before sliding it back into her military-style bun. "Am I being perfectly clear, Mr. Bowater?"

Feeling the threat as well as the full weight of what he had agreed to, the fat man wiped his head with dazed, somnambulant movements. He simply didn't know what to say. Worst of all, the distant ruckus of tourism could still be heard. The laughter of kids and good old boys fading behind the barks of a stringy-haired tee-shirt vendor.

Oblivious to it all was Mr. Boothe. He preferred it when Mrs. Nale took the lead with a client. It allowed him to concentrate on the scene. To listen to the silent story it was trying to tell. His eyes narrowed behind dark glass. Scouring the area for some detail--some overlooked clue that might prove of use.

He hadn't been involved with the installation--that simply wasn't his department. But the file on Project: Red Ridge was extensive, and despite what his longtime partner believed, he had read it many times. Included were numerous photos and video of the young specimen--from conception up to three months. Boothe had taken note of the bony nub on the snout and tiny, vestigial forelegs but for the most part, the thing had ended up looking a bit underwhelming. As far as he was concerned, it was just an ugly fish. Albeit one with hands.

Further growth was expected of course, but according to the report from bioengineering, the thing would end up being roughly the size of a very large sturgeon. Big enough for locals to see breaching and splashing around, but certainly not large enough to be a threat.

What he had called a slide, led down to a break in the trees, straight to the water's edge. This was framed on both sides by broken branches and brush. The gap hadn't been created by the specimen, but it had most definitely been widened by it.

Just beyond, dark water moved gently. Mr. Boothe watched it for a while, just lapping against a conspicuous rock which was placed dead center in the gap. It was sharp, curved like the dorsal fin of a shark and it rose four or five inches above the surface.

"Mr. Bowater?" Again came the pointed voice of Mrs. Nale. "I asked if you understand what I am telling you."

With this, the fat man seemed to recover a bit of gumption. He pulled out a short, sausage finger. "Hell yes I understand! You people are nothing but crooks! Swindlers! What do you take me for? Some empty-skulled, cow-tippin' hick? I'll have you know that while I may not have passed the Bar, I attended UMKC Law for five years. I know how to read a Goddamned contract. Beyond the initial fee, that financing option only kicks in if and when this monster of yours does what it's supposed to do. Puts this town back where it belongs--in the black. If that doesn't happen, the town of Red Ridge, Missouri isn't contractually obligated to do shit. You hear me, woman? I don't have to pay your fucking company another dime."

Mrs. Nale cleared her throat in a manner of overt politeness that felt to the fat politician like a middle finger straight up the old Hershey highway.

"*Mr. Bowater*," she asserted "While there is indeed a profit sharing component, that particular clause is rendered null and void in the event of a client requested removal of the specimen. I'm afraid, in that particular case, my employers would have no opportunity to recuperate their investment, thus leaving the purchasing party liable for the full cost... which as I'm sure you can recall from studying your contract so thoroughly, is quite considerable."

Walton J. Bowater had just about enough of this snotty Indian lady and her tone which practically dripped with condescension. In fact he was just about two words away from ringing her skinny, brown neck. Sure the big guy would probably club him over the back of the head before any real damage could be done. Probably turn his fat ass into fertilizer too... but that would be just as well. Better ending up as plant food than what the taxpayers of Red Ridge might do, if they found out the truth.

"Of course... there *is* one other option." The voice of Mrs. Nale had grown quiet.

"Is that right?" Bowater's teeth were audibly grinding. His fingernails digging into the swollen meat of his palms. "And what might that be?"

"Simply call off the removal."

The eyes of the Town Administrator went wide. His heart all but skipped a beat.

"Y-you mean..." Bowater stammered. "Just leave that damned thing where it is? Turn a blind eye as more people just..."

"Just *what*, Mr. Bowater?" The agent woman took a step closer--looking suddenly like a tiger. "Continue to talk? Continue to text and blog and Tweet? To arrive by car and busload from surrounding towns, states, one day even other countries perhaps--all with hungry eyes and loose wallets. Every man, woman and screaming child, desperate to catch a glimpse of *the Beast of Red Ridge, Missouri?*"

"Actually..." The fat man licked his lips. "Folk here call it the..."

"The croc-trout? Yes, I've seen the t-shirts--very classy." Mrs. Nale raised an eyebrow. "So, Mr. Bowater... what will it be? Shall my partner and I continue as planned? Capture your monster and erase all traces of its presence here? Or shall we leave your investment right where it belongs? Give it time to produce real fruit?" Again she smiled that tight, knife-like smile. "As always, the choice remains with the discretion of the client."

Bowater looked like a Polaroid left out too long in the sun. Like every bit of color had just drained to his feet. Behind glistening lips, his teeth worked. Grinding audibly as the conundrum was weighed. For an instant, the calls of the vendor man drifted back. He heard the first part anyway. The part about *rocking out.* After that though, things went a little nuts.

The event was sudden. Dramatic. It hit like a bomb going off. Where open air had been, now stretched a great wall of water, ten feet high. And shouting--there was definitely shouting.

The tall Indian man--what was his name? He was in the mud, on the ground, scrambling to get away from the face. The horrible impossible face that was halfway between a crocodile and the ugliest Goddamn fish Bowater had ever seen. Six foot long at least, and that was just the head! The Indian had a pistol in one hand and he was firing his pistol at the thing biting down on his leg. Curiously, the reports sounded more like the pops of bubble wrap than gunshots.

Enraged and apparently undamaged, the beast which locals had so eloquently named *the croc-trout,* opened its mouth to vomit forth a soundless roar. The force pushed hotly on the sweat-slick face of Walton J. Bowater and in that moment, he knew with all his heart exactly how Tom Dowdy must have felt, right at the end.

The woman was firing a pistol of her own now, but the bullets only bounced off the thing's skull--ricocheting in various directions. She was screaming something, that snotty bitch. Shouting over to her partner, or to what was left of him. The monster moved in short bursts, with a speed that belied its impressive bulk. Once more those long dinosaur jaws snapped shut and with a flick, the lower half of the Indian man just disappeared--painting the earth in a thick coat of red.

The eyes of the dying man reflected neither pain, nor shock, only a mild breed of confusion. When the animal's jaw snapped for a final time, conical teeth punched through the skull of Mr. Boothe and into his brain. After that, his eyes didn't reflect a damn thing.

The beast dragged itself farther up the embankment on stout forelimbs. Curiously, there were no hind legs, only a long bladed tail that looked transplanted from some monstrous eel. The flanks of the thing were scaly but not like a reptile's. These were fish scales. Light gleamed across every translucent facet as the top half of Mr. Boothe was swallowed in two swift gulps.

Distantly, Bowater realized that the woman had stopped firing. When he turned to look, it was like seeing through the haze of a dream. The woman stood, wavering in place, then stumbled back a step. One hand was clasped around her throat and her mouth was making strange shapes. For some reason, wet, gurgling sounds where the only sort she was able to make now. Bowater tried, but could make no sense of this.

There was a voice in the back of his brain. It was screaming. Grabbing him by the shoulders and shaking hard enough to give whiplash. RUN, YOU DAMNED IDIOT! The voice bellowed louder and louder. IT HASN'T NOTICED YOU! RUN WHILE YOU STILL CAN!

Mrs. Nale's knees gave out then. And with the last of her strength, the hand around her throat fell to reveal a high-pressured stream of blood. Apparently, one of her bullets had ricocheted almost perfectly--passing through her neck as if it hadn't been there at all. The initial spurt was the biggest--stretching a good ten or fifteen feet to spatter one of Bowater's custom Venetian loafers. But as she tumbled to the ground, a series of smaller streams shot from the wound--marking the trunks of trees with red slashes so bright, they seemed to glow.

As the fat politician watched the monster he had purchased drag itself past, he could no longer hear the voice in the back of his brain. In fact, the only sounds were coming from not so terribly far away. The ruckus of a town full of people--of whole families having grand old time. Everyone of them had come to catch a glimpse of something incredible. Something unbelievable.

"Sadie's... is booked to the end of the month." He informed the abominable amalgamation of fish and reptile. "Booked solid. For the first time since she can rightly remember. You believe that?" The croc-trout didn't answer. It simply swung its massive head so that one eye was aimed straight at the fat man's multiple, quivering chins.

Bowater took a step back, realizing that his vision had cleared some. The eye was hideous--milky. A gelatinous sack of yellow-grey jelly, crowned with an amorphous black stain. The pupil seemed to be leaking into the rest of the eye, like ink set in Vaseline. Bowater forced himself to look away. To concentrate on anything else, but a fetid wind forced itself into his nostrils and down his throat. The reek of the creature's breath forced the man back a step, but his heel connected with something. He stumbled. Fell right on his ass.

On impact, a stab of white pain exploded at the base of his spine. It was the man's favorite disk--good old number seven. He didn't need to be a chiropractor to know that. When Bowater opened his eyes again, he had to blink away tears. The croc-trout was still there. Still looking right back--the end of its snout barely two feet away now. It was then that he noticed something. Flat and curved like a two dimensional rhino horn, or maybe a wrongly-placed dorsal fin. The bony crest stuck up almost a full foot from the tip of the creature's snout and proved to be the very last thing that Walton J. Bowater ever saw.

"Rock out with your croc-trout?" The boy scratched his head. He couldn't have been more than seven or eight years old. "I don't get it."

"Hey, I'm not here to explain the jokes, kid." The tee-shirt vendor smirked, then pushed a greasy string of hair behind one ear. "You gonna buy something or what?"

The boy perused the contents of the table, rifling through a bowl of round button-style pins. There was only one design, but he liked it. A monstrous crocodile with a fish tail--really ugly. It looked like the scary boy-version of a mermaid. And unlike his baby sister, Sam Dunner *hated* mermaids.

"How much are the buttons?" He asked.

"Five dollars." Said the stringy-haired vendor man.

"Each?!" Repeated Sam. "Are you kidding? That's bullshit!"

"More like supply and demand, kid." The vendor shrugged his shoulders in a, *outta-my-hands* kind of way. "Look--I'll tell you what. The shirts are thirty. But if you buy one, I'll throw in a pin for nothing."

"Really?"

"Sure."

"Alright!" Blurted out the kid, unable to mask his excitement. *"I'll be right back! Just gotta ask my mom!"*

The vendor snickered, shook his head. Then he pulled out a fat wad of cash which he proceeded to count. "Hey, I'm here all day."

The boy raced around the beach, bobbing and weaving around people he didn't know. When he reached the picnic table his family had claimed for the afternoon, his mom was shouting at his little sister.

"Samuel!" She sounded exasperated. "Where the hell have you been? I told you half an hour ago we were leaving *in ten minutes*! Here." She shoved a tied up bag of trash against his chest. "Throw that away. There's a trash over there." She pointed to an old oil drum, back near the parking area.

"But *mom...*" Whined little Sam Dunner. "The guy with the shirts said that he--"

"I am not buying you a shirt, Samuel!" Marge Dunner said this in an all too familiar tone that Sam knew better than to argue with. "Your birthday is next month and you know we're meeting your daddy later for hot dogs. Right? Isn't that what you wanted?"

The kid looked crestfallen. "Yeah... I guess..."

"Okay then. Throw this out and get back here, *pronto*. We still have all your sister's toys to pick up. *Hear me?"*

"Yes, mama."

Sam walked slowly to the garbage. His back bent as if by the weight of some invisible burden. He tossed the bag, but it hit the rim--flopped onto the ground. And so, with the most exaggerated sigh he could muster, Sam Dunner tramped the rest of the way to the oil drum, snatched the bag off the ground and tossed it home.

That was when he saw it.

There was something in the dirt. A small white rectangle. Unable to turn away, the boy swiped it up, flipped it over. It was a business card, but there wasn't much on it. Just a drawing of what looked like a really weird fish--the kind he had seen once on an old pirate map. At least, he always assumed it had been a pirate map.

There was no address on the card. No phone number. Just a company logo and a tagline.

CRYPTIQUE: Designer Myths For a Modern Age

"Samuel Gerard Dunner!" Boy, his mom sure was in a mood. "Did you forget the *pronto* part?"

Spurred by a jolt of panic, Sam wiped his nose across one arm. Then he crammed the strange card into his pocket and ran for all he was worth.

Off Road

Tino had ridden down the middle of the road before, but never at such a breakneck speed. And never alone. Like all turns on this serpentine mountain thruway, the one up ahead was totally blind. Around it might be 18 wheels of unstoppable long-hauling destruction, or possibly just more road.

He peddled harder--leaning into the turn as the bike and boy seemed to merge. Squinting into the pre-dusk gloom, daring the headlights to manifest. The guard rail veered closer on his right and as he rounded that turn, Tino could feel a kind of gravitational pull. The drop-off beckoned always, but never more than in that moment. This was reckless riding but caution was a luxury he couldn't afford. If those four assholes caught up... the simple fact was, the Santino show wasn't gonna get another season.

Gravel exploded like buckshot from beneath the back tire as the purple bike rounded the curve. Waiting on the other side was no truck, no unstoppable destruction. Discovering this, Tino remembered to breathe again. The tunnel was in sight now. That was good. It meant he was almost to his hail Mary.

Maybe they gave up. He thought. Decided you ain't worth the effort.

The notion was nice but thoroughly unconvincing. Tino looked back to see a rider appear from around the bend.

"Shit." He cursed into the wind.

On his ass was none other than Gavin Labeck, first of his name, king douche of Creede High. Tino could still feel the catharsis of kicking that jerk in the balls. Sure wasn't the smartest thing he'd done since arriving in this one horse podunk... but that guy had it coming. And until fifteen minutes ago, he'd been about the farthest thing from Tino's mind. That was when something slapped him across the face causing the bike's front wheel to bang into a curb.

The resulting spill hadn't been pretty. Gathering himself and his bearings, it didn't take long to figure out what had happened. The partially eaten sandwich lay in pieces on the street and the jerks that had thrown it were walking their bikes his way.

"Aw, way to eat shit, Mosquito!" Called a voice.

Wiping the mustard from his face, the only thing Tino wanted was to get back on his purple Trek. Just ride home.

"Hey, don't be like that! You're so damn skinny, Will just wanted to share his ham and cheese."

"Sharing is caring, man." Card carrying lackey Will Fedders, chimed in right on cue.

"See?" Said Labeck with a snicker. "We're just watching out for ya, Mosquito. Making sure you get your three square meals. Come man, what do you say?"

"I say fuck you." The words were out before Tino could stop them.

The group guffawed at this, but their leader did not look amused. He was less than five steps away now.

"What did you just say to me?!"

Tino knew he had to act fast. Dropping what was left of his glasses, he hurriedly righted his bike

"Look, MOS-QUI-TO... I already told you we were just being friendly. And, if I heard right, a friend is exactly what you need these days. You know, since that stupid dog of yours got creamed."

For the first time in maybe ever... Santino looked his bully right in the eye.

"Damn. Wish I'd been there to see that," Labeck grinned. "I heard that mutt painted half the street."

That was it. Thought, speech, judgment--these systems were all offline. Santino Mosqueda had never been in a real fight before, but reason had given way to reflex. His foot shot out at full speed, smashing the kill switch between the jerk's legs, and that was pretty much that. The others could barely believe what they'd just seen. As such, it was a few seconds before they managed to pick either their jaws or their crumpled ringleader off the ground. As for the skinny kid from Detroit, all he was aware of was the pounding in his throat and fingers.

You idiot! What'd you do?!

Tino was already riding at full speed--tearing down the street like a purple missile. He didn't have to check behind. He knew it wouldn't be long before Labeck and his flock of assholes were riding straight up his skinny ass.

"Shit!" This was about the only word Tino could manage and he repeated it many times.

Pumping his legs for all they were worth, he banked hard at the end of the street and sped in the opposite direction of his only sanctuary. Home was behind him now. All the way at the end of Stoll Drive. Getting there would have meant turning around.

"Get back here you little shit bug!"

The shrill barks of Gavin Labeck were way too close for comfort. Already in full panic-mode, Tino could feel a cold tightness creeping across his chest. Over the past few months, he had mostly gotten used to the thin Colorado air, but going so fast for so long was starting to make him light headed. He didn't actually mean to take the left that led to the mountain pass. He was simply too busy focusing on not passing out to realize where he was headed. Soon enough though, the pitch of the ground asserted itself and he understood.

Oh good job, genius. Now you're really screwed. Ah well, maybe you'll pass out before they catch up.

Ahead, the mouth of a familiar tunnel yawned. Most kids in town never rode up the mountain, but Tino had been here many times--just him and Hiro. The cell reception was crap but you couldn't beat the views. Suddenly, a thought occurred. Something that would probably never work. A one in a zillion chance for escape.

With a sliver of newfound hope, Tino leaned in--bringing the darkness of the tunnel closer and closer. In a single rush of cold air, sound and light disappeared. In this new dimension, all he could hear was the buzzing whir of bike tires. First his own and then others.

"Nowhere to hide, MOSQUITO!!"

The voice exploded from all directions, bringing to mind the loud whooping calls of howler monkeys. Suddenly, Tino wished very much that he was on his couch. Watching National Geographic with the head of his best friend resting on one leg. Hiro was the size of a German shepherd and kinda looked like a wolf if you squinted hard. He was also the best dog in the entire universe. If not for him, Tino probably wouldn't have lasted a week, let alone six months in Wherever-The-Crap, Colorado.

It hadn't been anyone's fault. Not really. The dog had always listened before. Had always stayed with the bike--guarding it while Tino was in the store. There must have been a bird or squirrel. Something to make him run out like that. Even now, Tino could feel how his stomach had clenched. How he had stood there, frozen in place, no more useful than the car's headlights had been. It all happened in a flash. There was a blare of horn, a squeal of tires and then nothing. No yelp. No crying. For a second, Tino had actually thought the truck had miraculously passed through his best friend. But then he saw the blood.

"You know you can't ride forever!" Distantly, the lead howler monkey was whooping again. "You hear me... *ese*?!"

Though he tried to hide it from his parents, Tino really wasn't a fan of this place. Sure, the scenery was cool and the grocery store had a small rack for comics... but the locals held some seriously shitty ideas about people whose grandparents happened to be from Puerto Rico.

"When I catch you, you're dead! No one kicks me in the balls and lives!"

Labeck's words echoed all around but they didn't matter. What did was that he was going to reach the tunnel's exit a lot sooner than those jerks behind him were. They were big... but quick was better than strong. Back in Detroit there had been things to fly away from too. And with Hiro in tow, Tino had ridden hard across parking lots--down countless streets and alleys. Without knowing, he'd been honing his skills. Maybe for this very moment.

A second mouth yawned ahead--the yang to the previous yin. Like a bullet, Tino shot out of the tunnel into a world of punishing light. Using his eyes hurt for a second or two, but he squinted through the tears. Coming up was a massive bend. A scenic stretch for tourists to peek over the tops of a thick forest growing far below. Of course, driving by in a car it would be easy to miss the spot where the metal rail was incomplete. Or how certain branches had been snapped in such a way to fall and conceal the damage. Tino had noticed the spot two weeks back. At the time he hadn't dared go exploring but now his mind was fixated on nothing else. It was his only chance, his Hail Mary. He had to reach it before his pursuers had a chance to catch up.

Squeezing the brakes, the purple Trek skidded to a stop beside the snapped ends of guardrail. Something big had definitely crashed through-- probably one of those huge log-hauler trucks that took the mountain hairpins like they were straightaways. Whatever it was, the damage had been here for at least a couple of weeks.

"Man," Tino spat between heaving breaths. "If this was Detroit, the yellow tape would've been up in two minutes."

The purple Trek rocketed down the slope. Branches slashed at his face, but Tino never felt them. His eyes were wide, his knuckles white. Every riding skill had to be called upon just to keep the bike upright. Then to the boy's relief, the ground leveled out. Stopping in the leaf litter wasn't easy, but he managed-- allowing the purple Trek to fall on its side. Tino clasped a hand to his chest. He tried to catch his breath, but his chest felt like it was lined with razor blades.

"Damn. What's that?" He looked back up the slope toward the road. "Gotta be like three stories." He snickered. "Three stories on two wheels. I'll have to text Coop later. He's never gonna believe--"

A harsh rustling of leaves cut the thought. Something was running away.

"Shit." Tino's head darted around, trying to locate what had made the sound. "Probably just a squirrel." He licked his lips. "Just a really big freakin' squirrel."

Feeling the sudden need for a weapon, Tino snatched up a large stick. It was a good one--sturdy and not too long. In one swift motion, he brandished the thing like a samurai with a katana. After stealing one more look back where he'd come from, he swallowed hard.

"Well... come on Samurai. If they find you, it ain't gonna be here."

He turned to look in the opposite direction. Toward the broken trees and, presumably, the final resting place of whatever had punched through that railing. He moved slowly, cautiously--listening for any further rustlings or the voices of his pursuers. Gripping his katana tightly in one hand, Tino stepped onto what looked like an impact site. Stretching from this was a deep, conspicuous trench which he automatically began to follow. Sticks and broken branches lay atop freshly tilled soil and rocks that had probably not seen the light of day for centuries. And after a few steps more, Tino could see why.

Ahead was the overturned corpse of a truck--the kind fitted with a long silver tank on the back. The thing was huge, overturned and torn to absolute hell. Tino swallowed and pressed on with an almost superhuman level of caution. Suddenly it felt way too quiet down here. Like the trees were silently screaming at him to turn around and run. To just let the assholes back on the road have him.

"Galvani Electrical Refrigeration Inc."

Tino read the words aloud without really meaning to. The side of the tanker wasn't just busted, it was shredded. When close enough, he reached out to touch the edge of one of the ragged gashes. The metal was bent towards him. Almost as if something inside had clawed its way out.

"Oh, you haulin' Freon, Holmes? Yeah right," Tino sucked his teeth. "More like Weapon-X."

Seeing the gaping driver's compartment caused his expression to falter. While the rest of the vehicle was twisted on its side, the front had all wheels on the ground. Still, the driver side door hung open--attached by a single hinge. Tino swallowed hard, imagining what the remains of the vehicle's driver might look like after two weeks of exposure. Right then, he just wanted to run back to his bike, get back on the road and hope for the best.

Sniffing, he slapped a tear from his cheek and gripped his katana-stick just a little tighter. Then, with a shaky arm, he pulled himself up and squinted into the cab. It was empty. In a wave of relief, Tino let go of the breath he was holding and began to look around. The windshield was cracked but there were cuts in the seat leather. Long gashes that brought to mind the damage to the tanker outside... and the sort of nightmarish claws that could have made them. Worst of all was the blood. There were flecks of it on the exposed stuffing and the far window--more brown than red.

With a trembling hand, Tino tried to adjust his glasses. Then his heart sank.

"Aw, mom's gonna kill me." He moaned, remembering where he'd left them. Lying on the street--broken and covered in brown mustard. With a sigh, he pulled out his phone. A quick swipe of a thumb made the screen light up. Unsurprisingly, there were no bars, though he wasn't looking to make a call.

"7:42? Yup. You dead, Samurai. Dead and buried." He sighed, trying to imagine what he was going to say. "I know you told me not to lose another pair and all that but, it was all a big misunderstanding. See, these kids showed up from school and offered me a bite of their--"

BANG!

Something hit the side of the cabin then scrambled up onto the roof. A blur of shadow was all Tino saw through the passenger side window, but the thing was most definitely not a squirrel. Heart in throat, his eyes fell on the compartment behind the seats. Practically throwing himself in the back, Tino hunkered down beneath a small table, banging his head in the process.

"Shit." This was about the only word Santino could manage and he quietly repeated it many times.

When he opened his eyes again, they fell upon a mess on the floor. Amidst the empty Dorito bags and bottles of water, there were some very official looking papers, a business card with a company name below what looked like a sea monster. Still closer was a folder that sported the same logo as the card-- kind of an ugly fish with its tail in the air--the kind he'd seen on old maps. But instead of the company name, below the drawing was a single, eye-catching word stamped in red ink: CONFIDENTIAL.

TIK! TIK! CLIK! There was an ominous tapping on the roof. Idle click-clacks--like claws on metal. When the clicking stopped, there came a strange sliding sound, like something heavy being dragged. Tino didn't remember picking up the pass of papers, or why he was pressing them into his face. But after about a minute of silence, he began to read.

```
[SPECIMEN DESIGNATION] Tatzelwurm
[APPROX LIFESPAN] 280 days
[AGE AT INSTALLATION] 72 days
[NOTES] Specimen shows only minimal signs of
```

```
aggression.  Possible  burrowing  risk.  Install  on
hard,  mountainous  terrain  only.  Seems  to  exhibit
curiosity.  No  further  growth  expected.
```

Tino stared at the paper, his eyes sliding to the company logo on the folder itself.

```
CRYPTIQUE: Designer myths for a modern age
```

"Nope." Tino shook his head, whispering furiously. "No way. Uh-uh. *This ain't this.* This is just some stupid dream brought on by too damn many comic books. Right now, you in bed, Samurai. Sleeping off another Mountain Dew coma."

The words sounded true as he said them. Unfortunately, the something-currently-on-the-roof presented a convincing counterargument and slid off the other side of the roof. The same side as the gaping driver's door--still hanging by that one hinge. Tino swallowed, tried to remember even a single prayer that his Abuela had tried so hard to drill into his head.

But the broken driver side door was all he could look at. In some ways, the damned thing felt like everything he'd ever been afraid of. It was a gang of bullies. Oncoming headlights and the squeal of tires. It was moving away from home for Dad's new job and Abuela's last stroke and his goddamned diabetes getting worse. Because while Tino could see the open door, he couldn't do a Goddamned thing about it. Right then, Santino Mosqueda knew he was going to die in this place. Barely a hundred feet from the road, cowering in some long-haul truck driver's apartment.

Suddenly, like a crack of lightning, music banged into existence. The opening beats of "Daydreamin'" by Lupe Fiasco were so unexpected and startling, Tino's whole body flexed, bouncing his head off the table for the second time.

Daydream
I fell asleep beneath the flowers
For a couple of hours
On a beautiful day

* * *

His brain was spinning with too many sensations and partial thoughts. Through all of them, he could hear the song continue as if it were far away. Maybe underwater.

Daydream
I dream of you amid the flowers
For a couple of hours
Such a beautiful day

"Now I get signal? Now?!" The phone was outside, he realized. Involuntarily tossed and forgotten when he swan-dived into the back seat.

As I spy from behind my giant robot's eyes
I keep 'em happy cause I might fall out if he cries
Scared of heights, so I might pass out if he flies
Keep 'em on autopilot cause I can't drive

The music stopped. Everything stopped. Santino couldn't breathe and he didn't dare look away from the door he had no way of closing. He could hear the strange second sound. No longer above but beside him. Like someone was dragging a body around the front of the truck. He had to do something, but what? Santino had never had to defend himself before. That had always been Hiro's job.

"Hiro."

Tino's eyes welled up. He could almost hear him barking, panting, sniffing for forgotten snacks under the bed. In fact, he could hear those exact sounds right now. Just outside, just below the door... a deep sniffing, snuffling--the breath of something big. Hands clamped over his mouth, Tino watched in horror as a crest of thick black fur came into view. A bear was his first thought, but then he saw the tail. Long and tufted like a lion's, it swayed back and forth in the opening of the driver's side door. Then it shot forward, slapping the seat.

"Yo! Yo! Mosquito!" The voice came from the direction of the road. "I know you're down here! We found your stupid girl bike!"

Labeck's shouting had an immediate effect on whatever was investigating the cell phone. The tufted tail disappeared as whatever was attached to it took off. Tino tracked the rustling sounds as they skittered back around the other side of the truck and into the brush.

"Oh come on, *ese*!" The voice was louder, closer. "You didn't really think we were gonna just give up and go home, did you?!"

Tino had never been so afraid in his entire life. And yet, in that moment he realized something. Whatever fear he was experiencing wasn't for those jerks from school. He took a deep breath. Then, after sliding out from his hiding spot he snatched the stick off of the seat. He jumped from the driver's seat, careful not to land on his phone. The screen was dark, but his index finger instinctively moved to light it up.

1 Missed Call (Mom)--said the message on the lock screen.

"*Hey, over there! He's in the truck*!" Shouted someone. The rest all turned, looking as ugly and stupid as ever.

"Guys," Tino frowned, gripping his wooden sword as hard as he could. "Hold up! Listen to me! There's something down here. Something... big. We gotta get outta here."

Gavin Labeck snickered, inspiring his cronies to do the same. "Wow, that is fucking precious. Really. What'd you see a bear when you were hiding in that truck, Mosquito?"

"Ain't no bear, man."

"Of course there isn't. You just think I'm stupid, ain't that right?"

"Naw, man. Come on, it aint like that." Tino sighed--realizing that there'd be no convincing anyone of what he'd just experienced, least of all these assholes. "Look..." He scanned the surroundings for anything big and hairy. "You got me, I got you back. That's all."

"Ohhh, and you think that's how things work around here, Mos-qui-to? The only give and take around here is what I give and what you take." Still grinning, he gave the much smaller kid a firm shove. "That doesn't happen, well... what I give is gonna get worse. Comprende?"

Tino made a sucking noise with his teeth. He was less than ten feet from the bullies who had flicked his last nerve.

"Bitch please." He turned to regard the truck. "Calling me Mosquito all the time, when you the one walkin' round with that breath. Maybe do us all a favor and brush your teeth with something besides dog shit."

Despite themselves, the three cronies chuckled at this.

"Dog shit?" Labeck stepped forward and thrust a closed fist into Santino's stomach. "Dog shit?!" After pulling off his belt, he wrapped it around Tino's neck and squeezed. "You know who you're talking to?! Huh!? Let's see who's full of dog shit now! I'll squeeze it out of ya!!"

Shocked by the sudden violence, the other boys backed off a step. Will Fedders seemed about to protest... but something else caught his eye. Something long and black on top of the ruined tanker and a hell of a lot scarier than Gavin Labeck. Will's eyes followed the inexplicable thing that looked like the back end of a hairy anaconda. It was waving back and forth like a metronome, keeping time with his pounding heart.

Frantically, Tino struggled against the belt around his neck. Pulling, battling, wishing he was strong enough to do terrible and righteous things to his attacker. The light of the world was starting to fade and with it all sounds. In fact, he was only vaguely aware of the sudden rustling--like something huge charging through the brush and the leaves.

What happened next, happened all at once. An impact... a return of light and sound and air... a whip-flash of something dark... and the sight of the biggest asshole in town flying face first into the dirt. All of these things coalesced in Tino's experience into a single conglomerate blur of relief. Unable to stop himself, the boy pitched forward, expelling cough after cough into the ground. For many long seconds, he remained oblivious to the carnage going on around him.

Without his glasses, Tino had to squint to bring what he was looking at into some semblance of focus. The creature whose jaws were clamped around Will Fedders' neck glared in warning as it growled softly. Here was what the truck had been hauling and, as Tino has previously surmised, it most definitely was not Freon. The front half was pure panther complete with a snarling cat-like head and two front legs which ended in massive paws. The mismatched back-half was that of an enormous snake--fifteen feet long or more. A long legless tube covered in black fur that tapered down to the tufted tip he had glimpsed earlier. Though the presence of such a beast was enough to send sanity packing, Santino Mosqueda never thought of turning away.

Panther-snake. Tatzelwurm.

The names ran through Tino's head and they were followed by one more. A label that felt most correct.

Weapon-X.

The thing was clutching one of the boys in its mouth. The same one who has thrown the sandwich. Will Fedders was looking right at Tino. His skin had faded to a sickly gray and for some reason, he was spending his last few moments of life on a hopeless, wordless plea.

Help me, said those pitiable eyes. Whatever we did--whatever we were going to do... you gotta help me now. We don't deserve this. No one deserves this.

Hearing every unspoken word, Tino stared right back. He watched expressionless, as the long snake-like tail coiled further around Will's chest--tightening, constricting until the boy's cheeks turned inward--becoming caverns in his skull.

As for the king douche of Creede High, at first, all he could do was gape and stare like his brain had fallen out. Then, seeing two of his cronies had already done the same, he promptly started to run.

"Yo! Asshole!"

Labeck turned to look but the stick was already in mid-swing. After that, all he knew was light and pain. When he hit the ground, one leg hit funny and bent the wrong way. By the time he stopped rolling, there was dirt in his mouth, blood on one knee and all he could do was make noises like a wounded puppy.

Suddenly horrified by what he'd just done, Santino looked over at the not-Freon and it looked right back. Yellow eyes flitting back and forth between the boy with the stick and the crumpled one who was whimpering softly on the ground. At last, the beast opened its mouth--sliding two venomous saber-fangs out of the cold throat of Will Fedders. The withered husk dropped to the ground, making a straw-like crunch that made Tino want to throw up.

"I'm sorry!" Tino blurted out, unsure who he was apologizing to. Right then he wanted to run but his legs felt like unbendable sticks. As the panther-snake half walked, half slithered towards him, all Tino knew was that he'd backed the wrong horse. And worse, that he would never hear the voice of his mother again. Tears streaming down his face, the boy from Detroit closed his eyes and sang along to the Lupe Fiasco song playing in his head.

"Daydream... I fell asleep beneath the flowers... For a couple of hours... On a beautiful day." There were rustling footsteps followed by the sound of something heavy being dragged. "Daydream... I dream of you amid the flowers... For a couple of hours... Such a beautiful--"

The sound of teeth entering flesh was unmistakable. Santino opened his eyes just as the fur-covered snake-half insinuated itself around Labeck's busted leg. The beast was pulling the body closer--claiming it. Warning the singing boy with an unbroken stare as it began its second course.

Like a crack of lightning, Tino took off. Capitalizing on the moment, he ran for all he was worth--as far away from the shredded truck and the creature that couldn't possibly exist but was definitely draining the life out of the biggest asshole he had ever met. When he came to the collection of discarded bikes, he grabbed his purple Trek and kept going. Heading straight for the slope and the mountain road that would lead him back...

But there was something around his foot. Something long and black and covered in fur. Frantically, Tino fought to pull free but in one tremendous jerk, he was yanked into the air. The face appeared suddenly and it was upside-down. The boy wanted to close his eyes, but couldn't remember how. So he watched. Waiting for the teeth to appear again.

"Well?" Santino's voice was remarkably calm. "Go on! Do it already!!"

The eyes were the most yellow things he had ever seen. Slitted and indifferent like those of a house cat. When the mouth opened, fangs unfolded from the roof of the mouth. Anchored by fleshy gums, the teeth reached outward.

"I... fell asleep beneath the flowers" Santino's singing was forgivably off key, given the circumstances. "For a couple of hours... on a beautiful day." It was then that Tino realized he wasn't so much singing, as singing along. He could feel the beats--could actually hear Fiasco doing his thing. He stopped, opened his eyes to see that the panther face was no longer staring at him, but at a glowing rectangle on the floor. The screen said two words: Mom Calling.

Suddenly, the ground rushed upwards. The landing wasn't pleasant but

Tino recovered fast. He had no choice. No chances left. Reaching out, he grabbed the phone, sliding a thumb across the screen.

"Mom? Hey!" Santino felt an overwhelming swell of emotion but he fought to stay cool. Across his throat was the ghost of Labeck's belt, but he cleared his throat and forced the words out. "Oh... nothing much. I just went for a ride up the mountain and forgot my water. Throat's a little dry is all. I'm fine."

Tino sat up, looked over at the... what had the paper in the truck called it? The thing looked confused--crooking its head to one side, just like Hiro used to.

"No, I'm... good, mom. Really. It's just... I fell off my bike. No I'm okay really but... my glasses? They're toast."

Tino held the phone away from his ear as his mom reacted to this. The tatzelwurm was moving again. Dragging its lower half around in a circle until it was coiled like a furry garden hose. Then it opened its mouth far wider than feline jaws should be able to and released a yawn.

"Okay, okay. Yeah, I know. I promise I'll be more careful." Tino looked down. The end of the creature's tail was close enough to touch. "I just wanna... hang back here a few more minutes. Catch the sunset. Ok. Yeah. Uh huh. Love you, mom. Dad too. Tell him, okay? Tell him... I'll be home soon."

Santino pressed the phone to his chest and unleashed a sigh. Talking had hurt like hell, but hearing the voice of his mother had been worth every second. This time, when the tears came, he didn't fight them. The last thing he said to her kept running through his mind. The part about being home soon... had that just been a pretty lie?

Tino looked at the bodies of his pursuers. There were only two. The others must have gotten away when the thing was preoccupied. As for Gavin Labeck and Will Fedders, neither was recognizable. They looked like thousand year old mummies.

"So..." Tino said tentatively. "You like them beats?" After powering up his phone again, he pressed the screen a few times until the same song started playing again. This sparked a reaction in the chimeric beast. A kind of chainsaw grinding which came from deep in its mismatched body.

"Oh shit, you pur?!" Tino chuckled in spite of himself. "Tell you what. I'mma call you X. That cool?"

Again, Tino glanced at the pair of dried out husks who had chased him here not half an hour ago. The fact was, he couldn't know if the thing that had killed them was going to let him leave this place. But this was a problem that felt different than the broken door he couldn't close or the diabetes. In fact, as the beats continued to flow from his phone, Tino had the distinct impression that he was doing... something.

Monster whispering. The term pulsed in his brain.

"You know I never been that into cats, but hey--I never tried sushi before last year and that shit is fucking delicious." The tatzelwurm did not respond. In fact, it appeared to be asleep. Reaching out a hand, Tino gingerly stroked its tail. The fur was thick and soft and for the first time in many days, he didn't feel alone.

ROOSTER

ZANDAXARR

With a weary exhalation, Bert put down the copy of Kerrang magazine he was pretending to read. As it turned out, 'The Night Alice Knocked 'em Dead in Detroit' had proved more depressing than anything. Sure, the concert looked to have been a hell of a time. But it was just another in a long line of articles which proved how much fun other young people really had. People who weren't Bertram Mancini.

The simple fact was, when all your best life experiences leaped off a printed page, there was a limit to how much you could stomach before resentment came knocking.

"Shit." Grumbled Bert, sliding the magazine across the counter. "It's not like you can expect Alice Cooper to set foot in a shit-hole like this."

However harsh Bert's assessment might have been, Bessimer, Michigan was as far from Detroit as you could get without leaving the state. Nine hours as the crow flies. Sure it was the only home Bert had ever known, but to him, the town felt more like a prison. Especially on Saturdays. The last day of a seven day cycle he was doomed to eternally repeat.

He looked past the front counter--out to the noisy machines and empty rows. Besides himself there was only one other person left in the Lazer Blade Arcade. And of course, it was that same guy in the red hoodie. Bert had never heard his real name, but you didn't need to be Batman to decipher the letters 'J

O K R'. From day one, it had felt like there was something off about the guy. After all... what grown-ass man spends their Saturday nights alone in a shitty arcade? As Bert wondered this, a wave of cold irony caused him to release a defeated sigh.

He looked at his watch and frowned. 10:40.

Bessemer wasn't exactly what you'd call a cultural hotspot of the modern age. Fact was, if you were a young person looking for good times after dark, your options were on the slim side. Those hoping to catch the latest Stallone flick, had better know someone with a ride because the closest theater was two towns over. Of course there was always the local passtime of drinking and passing out. But since Congress hadn't pulled their heads out of their asses back in '84, you had to be over 21 to play. And so it happened that a local entrepreneur called Tom Kramer had purchased and filled a shitty old warehouse with an array of various electronic games and pinballs. Converting it into a flashing neon welcome sign for the town's disaffected youth.

By 7pm on weekends, the Lazer Blade was always packed. Filled with loud shouts and laughter which added to the endless bleeps, bloops and the roar of digitized explosions. The regulars were all just stupid kids but they were okay. Bert liked to think of them as the rabble. Whenever one tried to bug him, he would just pretend to be busier than he actually was. This was for the best. Becoming too friendly would erode that clear line of delineation he had worked so hard to build.

Bert was the man in charge, the Key-Master--the only person in the Lazer Blade with the power to investigate after a quarter had been eaten or if the little cups of the skeeball had been filled with one or more bodily fluids. No--he was decidedly not one of them. And while he did share the rabble's passion for video games, Bert liked to play after hours. When he could actually, finally concentrate.

From behind the counter he glared at the guy in the red hoodie. The dude was tall--built like a giant novelty pencil. For three months he had been coming in on Saturday nights--always alone, always dropping all his quarters into that one machine. And whenever the guy was the last one to leave, Bert always found himself checking his watch a little more frequently.

Again he looked down. 10:43. Close enough.

"Hey," Bert's voice cut through the conglomerate digital symphony. "Fifteen minutes."

After saying this, Bert watched the back of the guy's head--hoping for a turn, a nod... any sign of comprehension. The silhouette was rimmed in flashing blue light from the monitor. Same guy, same hoodie and as always, he was playing that same game. Bert's game.

ZANDAXARR was regarded by many amidst the rabble to be one of the most brutally difficult games in the arcade. But for some reason, whenever Bert wrapped his fingers around that blood red joystick, something just clicked. He didn't just play ZANDAXARR, he became it. In a way, actually inhabiting that pixelated world of tooth and claw. It was the one place that he didn't just visit, but rule. And everyone in the Lazer Blade knew it. To those lesser mortals, Bert was a golden blood-spattered god. Problem was, for the last three months, a challenger had been actively seeking to dethrone him. JOKR. The name emblazoned upon a list of Top Warriors and on Bert's very soul.

"It's fine," He thought. "No sweat. Only a couple more minutes. Just start shutting off the lights, grab a smoke and by the time you get back, he'll be gone. And then, that red joystick is all yours."

Upon reaching the back door, Bert pulled out a ring of keys but dropped them. Splashing down to the concrete floor, these proceeded to slide under a non working pinball table. Bert sighed, then bent down to look. Beneath the machine, his nose crinkled at the bouquet of stale beer and piss. He could see the keys, but they had slid all the way against the wall.

"Of fucking course," he grumbled, looking for something to help lengthen his reach. There was usually a broom back here, but it was nowhere to be seen. Suddenly, Bert remembered something. Odds were, that particular broom was still leaning up against the wall outside Mr. Kramer's office... all the way on the other side of the warehouse... exactly where he had left it.

With an audible groan, Bert went flat onto his stomach and extended a leg under the broken machine. With the toe of his shoe, he began to feel around until he was able to locate the key ring. It was then that he heard it. The chime of the bell that meant the front door had just been used.

It was a sound so wonderful, despite being on the floor and on his stomach... despite being surrounded by smells he wished he could forget, Bert felt a wave of blissful relief. JOKR was gone.

What was that line from The Goonies?

"This is our time, Mikey. Our time." Keys in hand, Bert straightened up and pulled out his pack of Camels. "Three left." He shrugged. "Have to hit Chen's in the morning."

Right then he could practically taste those lemon pastry things that Mrs. Chen made on Sunday mornings. And for that one fleeting moment, Bert felt pretty alright.

"HOLY SHIIIIT!"

The exclamation came with all the subtlety of a thunderclap. Clutching his chest, Bert turned back to stare into the empty rows of flashing cabinets as his stomach sank. It was JOKR. Had to be. For months the son of a bitch hadn't said a word, but something had just made him cuss loud enough to knock the Lazer Blade's night manager half out of his skin. And now, the son of a bitch was starting to laugh.

Bert tried to control his breathing. What was his problem? He was twenty-six, not forty-six. So why the hell did his heart feel like it was two beats aways from an attack? What did he have to be afraid of?

The cackling was filling the room, but this was no joyous sound. The longer Bert listened, the more it sounded like venom. Like spite.

He *had* heard the front door, hadn't he? Yes. Definitely. Even amidst the racket of all the video games, it was unmistakable. But if JOKR was still here... had someone else come in?

Bert checked his watch with wide, hungry eyes. 10:50.

Holding harder onto the key ring than before, he finished locking up the back door, then flipped a series of switches that made the right half of the Lazer Blade fall into darkness. That would do the trick. Whoever was in here with him couldn't possibly ignore the lights cutting out like that. Pretty soon he'd hear the chime of that front bell again. Absolutely. For sure. Any second now.

Bert moved slowly past the rows of games with their dark, sleeping monitors. Cautiously making his way towards the maniacal celebrations as his heart continued to pound. Irrationally, he wished he had some kind of weapon. A broom maybe... or a double-bladed axe that shot bolts of lighting out the front.

As he rounded the final row and came to where his counter and register were, Bert turned his head to the right. His eyes fell on ZANDAXARR and the guy in the red hoodie. By this point, the laughter had died off. Currently, JOKR was just standing there with arms folded, staring at the screen.

Bert made a gulping sound with his throat.

"Hey," He called out in the firmest voice he could muster. "Didn't you hear me? Didn't you see the lights? We're closed."

Bert waited for a response but none came. And so he began to move again, this time to his final, inevitable destination.

"Hey buddy. You deaf? I said--"

"Yeah, yeah. I heard you." JOKR's voice was deep. "I'll get outta here in a second, but first... you gotta see this."

Bert nervously licked his lips. None of this felt right. Before now, he and the kid in the red hoodie had never spoken. In fact, when he wasn't staring into a monitor, JOKR seemed intent on studying the floor as he walked, keeping both hands in his pockets. There was never eye contact, nor even a nod as he passed. And now, two minutes past closing time on the coldest Goddamned Saturday of October, he wanted to *show* Bert something?

Step after step brought the master of ZANDAXARR closer and closer to the man who had stepped up to challenge his claim to the throne. The would-be usurper. Bert kept waiting for the guy to turn around, but his back and shoulders remained firm. Suddenly, Bert realized something. He had always thought of JOKR as tall and so incredibly thin. But now that only a couple of steps separated them, he could see they were almost the same height.

"Check it out," JOKR's voice oozed, sounding damn pleased with himself.

Bert took another step, sparing a glance for the game's marquee, which glowered right back. The artwork featured the word ZANDAXARR in bold letters that were getting struck by lightning. On the left side was the face of the heroic Zan. Your typical shirtless Conan rip-off but with long red hair. On the right side was a similar character, but with some distinct alterations. Red skin, white hair with solid yellow eyes and a mouthful of demonic fangs. A novice might assume the two faces represented the hero and villain of the game, but the reality was so much cooler than that.

One final step brought Bert directly aside of the man he knew only as JOKR. Stealthily, he stole a quick glance at the kid's face, but the red hood obscured all but the very tips of a nose and chin. Painted by the flickering monitor light, it was impossible to tell if the guy was white, black, brown or green with yellow polka dots.

Warily, Bert looked at the screen of his favorite game. Currently, it was in attract mode--playing out a bit of pre-recorded gameplay. After a few seconds, everything went black, and then it happened. A huge double-bladed axe crashed down and was promptly struck by lightning. Then two words appeared. 'ZAN' and 'DAXARR'. One white, one red--one good, the other evil. Without warning, these raced towards one another, crashing into the center of the axe to be hit by a final bolt of digital lightning. When the light and sound had faded away, it was revealed that the two words had become one.

"ZANDAXARR." Bert heard the word in his mind as he gazed upon the pixelated golden letters he had seen a thousand times before.

"So what am I supposed to see?" Bert asked as if he didn't already know.

"Wait for it." Said JOKR, as the screen again cut to black.

The next few seconds were horrible. They seemed to stretch and distort in Bert's stomach. Right then, he wished he could reach the power cable with his foot. Somehow unplug the machine before the next screen became real.

"Hey, a couple minutes ago... did you hear the door? The front bell?" Bert sounded exactly like someone trying to change the subject. "Did anyone else come into the arcade? Cause we're closed. Everyone needs to get out of here so I can finish locking up and..."

"And what?" Said JOKR. "Make sweet sweet love to that lady you got waiting for ya back home? You know, I heard of kissing cousins... but your own grandma? Shit, man... she can wait."

Bert's stomach hit the floor and kept going. He couldn't think, couldn't blink. Even breathing was impossible because the air felt like it was made of knives. The simple fact was... no one knew he lived with his grandmother. Not the rabble. Not Mr. Kramer.   It wasn't exactly the sort of detail you go spreading around for street cred.

In shock, his eyes drifted back to the screen, ZANDAXARR was playing out another of its three stages. The one where all the castles were replaced by volcanos. Bert could only watch as the little barbarian moved along his preordained path towards the stone idol in the center of the screen. As soon as the icon had been collected, the screen flashed, and the heroic Zan was transformed. Replaced by a red skinned version of the character who proceeded to unleash a barrage of lighting from his double-bladed axe. Seeing this flipped a hidden switch inside the night manager of the Lazer Blade Arcade.

"What the fuck did you just say?" Bert's voice was different. More sure of itself. Less burdened by things like anxiety or give-a-fuck. He was ready to go on when the screen went dark again.

"You ready, B-Man?" The excitement in JOKR's voice was plain. "Don't wanna miss this."

When the screen lit up again, it might as well have contained all the light in the universe. Here it was, the source of his golden-Godhood. The proof that Bert Mancini was not only separate from the rabble, but above them. Line after line appeared--populating a list of what the large text at the top proclaimed to be 'THE TOP WARRIORS'. There were ten slots, each displaying four characters and a corresponding score.

```
 1.  BMAN     66,312
 2.  BMAN     64,643
 3.  BMAN     63,273
 4.  BMAN     59,235
 5.  BMAN     59,018
 6.  BMAN     57,864
 7.  BMAN     55,993
 8.  BMAN     55,843
 9.  BMAN     54,524
10.  JOKR     53,467
```

"So what do you think?" Said the guy in the red hoodie.

Bert looked confused. He blinked dumbly, then looked again. Willing the screen not to change, he re-scanned the names.

"Tell you *what*, B-Man... this game isn't half as hard as they say," The kid snickered. "Everyone talks about ZANDAXARR like it's worse than Ghosts and Goblins but I scored 4th place on my first try."

"First try? " Bert took a step back then shook his head. "You're full of shit, kid. You've been in here playing the game for weeks. Christ, I've even seen your name on the board before. You placed last month too. You're the fucking Joker."

"That's not my name," The kid's voice had turned sharp, but after a few tense moments of silence, it softened again. "Anyway, I bet that stung. Seeing a name besides yours on that list? Not at the bottom or anything, but in the top five? Shit, that must have driven you practically crazy. I mean it's not like you have anything else going on, right?"

"Hey! Screw you, you little shit!" Bert's anger flared. "Just... get the hell out of here. It's late."

"Well, you're right about that. It is late, B-Man. Way too late." The kid shoved his hands in his pockets as if he was making sure he had everything with him before heading out. "It took you a whole month to knock my score down from 4th to 10th place?"

Bert glared, saying nothing.

"I would have thought a *master player* like you would've been able to get rid of the evidence quicker than *that*." The kid shrugged, "Still, I'm thinking tonight's the night. What about you? I mean all you gotta do is place anywhere on that list and I'll be erased forever. Like I was never here. Isn't that what you want, B-Man? What you've been trying to do since I first threatened this pathetic house of cards you call a rep?"

"That's it." Bert slammed a hand down on the kid's shoulder, spun him around. "Look! I don't want to see you in here again. You hear me?"

The kid didn't look up. He just kept staring at the floor. "I'll leave as soon as you say my name, B-Man."

"What? Why the fuck would I know your name? All I got is four letters. J-O-K-R."

"That's not my fucking name and you know it." The voice echoed from within the cavernous void of the kid's hood.

"What? No... I don't know shit!!"

"Sure you do, B-Man. Look, there's no point in lying. Not to me. We both know perfectly well what you did."

Every bit of color drained from the face of Bertram Mancini. It was like someone had flipped a switch. Suddenly frantic, he clapped both hands over his ears as his mind raced to a dozen places at once. Home, Nana's basement, his stool, the front counter, Mrs Chen's, the baseball bat Mr. Kramer kept under the front counter.

"You're wrong!" He screamed. "I don't know you! I don't know shit! *I don't know shit!!*"

As he ran, Bert focused only on the bat. The counter was reached in a matter of seconds and he rounded it too fast, banging his hip on one corner. Wincing from the pain, he dropped, reached underneath... but the Louisville Slugger was gone.

"What are you looking for?" The voice in his ears was grinning. It sounded different than before. Higher in pitch. Younger. "Nothing there. What--did you forget or something? You never put it back."

"How? How could you know that?" Bert spun round to see a silhouette wreathed in flickering monitor light. The red hoodie was there, but the person was smaller than the one he had left standing next to ZANDAXARR. JOKR had been taller than Bert, but this... this was just a kid. Twelve or thirteen, tops. And he was walking very slowly, holding something long in one hand.

"You could have just unplugged it, you know."

"No!" Bert was trembling. Behind the counter, his back was already pressed against the wall.

"Oh right, right. That would have restored the factory settings. Thrown out the baby with the bathwater. And I bet that Warrior List took forever to fill up, didn't it? Years probably. But then, what else is there to do in a shit-hole town like this? And being such a pathetic fucking loser, I mean... it's not like you got anything else going on."

Finally, the kid threw back his hood and stepped into the light. Once Bert could see his face, it all came flooding back. Everything he had tried to hard to bury. The curly brown hair and sad eyes. The scarred upper lip. That face had been all over the newspapers for weeks. Joey Kerrigan. Age 12. Last seen by his mother, who had sent him to the Bessemer Laundromat on August 11th, 1986.

The papers mentioned that Joey didn't have many friends. And that sometimes, in between the wash and dry cycles, he would cross the street to play a few rounds of his favorite game at the local arcade.

With tears streaming down his face, Bert looked up from where he sat in the puddle of his own making. The kid looked just like he had that night. Only now, with the hood down, a cavernous indent was visible on the side of his skull. There was blood glistening there. Running down his cheek and neck as if freshly freed. Worse was the little shit's smile. It was too wide, filled with too many teeth. Stretching the scar left by the surgery that had joined the boy's cleft lip and palate.

Gripping the end with both hands, the ghost of Joey Kerrigan raised the baseball bat high into the air. "Not exactly a fucking lightning axe, but it did the trick last time, am I right?"

"I..." Bert's words felt like knives as they left his throat. "Kid... please... I'm so fucking sorry."

"No argument here, B-Man. Even I didn't go out in a lake of piss."

The bat flew and Bertram screamed. Screamed until he couldn't remember the where, the why or who the man running towards him was.

"Bert?" Mr. Kramer was standing not two feet from the spot where his night manager was apparently having a fit on the floor. "Jesus, Bert! What the hell!? What'd you do?!"

When officers finally arrived on scene, an extremely shaken Tom Kramer told them the truth. He had arrived just 10 minutes before the incident--right before closing. He had gone straight to his back office, apparently to retrieve an overdue electric bill. When he returned to the front counter area, Mr. Kramer discovered an employee by the name of Bertram Mancini furiously smashing his own face with a blood-soaked Louisville Slugger.

THE TERROR OF LONDON

The Terror of London

The drawing room was still, and it was dark. Within lurked a near perfect silence, broken only by the steady machinations of a nearby clock.

The old man turned to regard the ticking thing which cared little for his solitude. But the face of the grandfather clock was obscured--swallowed by the darkness of the hour. Once again, nothing could be discerned beyond the obvious. The hour was late. Very late indeed.

What little light there was came from a brass candelabra. Unmolested by breath or by draft, its three candle-flames glowed like strange ethereal things, but they could not hold the old man's gaze. This slid down the flickering shaft, onto the surface of a most impressive desk. The Bureau Mazarin was a piece fit for a Duke. It had been imported all the way from France, long before its current owner was born. Like most things in Covington Manor, the red and gold desk was usually immaculate, pristine. Before tonight, it had never known the touch of blood. Absently, a wrinkled hand pushed something out of the light. Something curved and pale that might have been bone.

In the shadows, framed portraits and statuary from around the world were displayed on tables and shelves, or hanging beside book-lined walls. The surroundings spoke of worldly travels and rare privilege, but to the room's only occupant, such bric-a-brac was worthless. John Arthur Covington was a man who yearned for one thing--to once again feel adrenaline coursing through the useless withered sticks that had once been his legs.

John's formative years provided little enough time for anything beyond the retracing of well-established footsteps. He was his father's son, after all. The heir to a long line of healers that stretched four generations into the city's past. Duty and family weighed quite a lot, but there was nothing to be done. John was a good son and had become a fine upstanding member of society--another stalwart Covington for queen and country. And if the man were secretly dead inside, such crosses were his alone to bare.

A curious thing occurred on the day he first loomed over a living subject-- the cold power of a scalpel in one hand. In that moment, John Covington had discovered his first taste of true thrill. Not the sort described on a written page, but the real thing. The sort the heart pumps to one's every nerve and sinew.

Of course, a surgeon's work was nothing if not bloody, but its potential woke something deep inside the young man. Something primal. Whether it was the prospect of saving lives or of plunging steel into warm flesh, the yearning that had plagued him since boyhood seemed satisfied. The life of a surgeon might be no proper adventure, but there were certainly worse fates.

Thinking of those days made the old man's lips curl.

Such times seemed impossibly distant--less memory and more half-forgotten dream. With a twitch, John slid his wrinkled hands to the tops of large wheels. One on each side. The chair was a rolling chaise--an Alderman No. 9. The latest in a long line of state of the art mobile prisons.

A single push set the device in motion. Its large wheels carried the current patriarch of the Covington line across the drawing room. Ambivalently, John glanced up to where the bottom edge of a frame could be discerned, though he didn't need to see the painted eyes of his great grandfather to know they did not approve.

The Covington line had been an affluent one for at least five generations. Doctors, surgeons--men of science, all working to better the lives of the miserable and afflicted. All, that is, except for the one Covington who, after passing his final exam, decided that racing his horse down the steepest hill in Sussex would be a cracking good way to celebrate. Unfortunately, the grey thoroughbred hadn't taken more than four steps before snapping an ankle. Rather than being thrown, the rider had remained in his saddle the entire way down the hill. In fact, if classmate Tom Rutherford had not been along to witness the stunt, John would surely have died. Bent, broken and pinned beneath ninety stone of demised thoroughbred.

The great Dr. Bernard Covington had insisted on performing all of his son's surgeries personally. Though if God himself had held the scalpel, the result would have been no different.

To the old man's recollection, it had been around that time that the Covington portraits had begun to glare. John looked into the darkness above, to the very spot he knew his great grandfather's eyes were. He would not suffer their faces for much longer. Very soon he would leave on one last grand adventure. One final jaunt before the bill came due. After that, his relatives could look down their noses at whoever the hell they liked.

The Alderman chair rolled to a stop before a very large window. The moon was of little help, but such limited visibility could hardly stop John from seeing the view. Most of his adult life had been spent absorbing that garden, that fence, that cobbled street. He could feel them even now, burning beneath his dead heels.

Lazily, John turned again to the south wall, where the grandfather clock ticked and ticked and told him nothing. With ease, thumb and forefinger found particular spots on a hairless scalp remembering ancient, long gone aches. The pain existed only in echoes now, but it was real. His thumbs traced tiny circles, feeling the ticks of the clock pulse beneath his paper skin.

Seventy-nine. God, how could he have gotten so old? With a weary sigh, John's eyes meandered to a small Bombay cabinet, just barely outlined in candlelight. Though it was not visible in the dark, he stared at a tiny keyhole which was set into the cabinet's only drawer.

From a pocket, a sizable keyring was produced. There were more than two dozen keys, though most were fairly small. As it happened, in Covington manor, doors were not the only things which required their touch. In such place, there were too many secrets. Too many little disgraces to hide from prying eyes.

With a subtle key-turn click, John slid the drawer open. Inside lay a stack of literature--though calling them such felt wrong. Something like honoring a crow by dressing it for Christmas dinner. Dreadfuls, the common folk called them--an affectation which made clever reference to both subject matter of the publications as well as their overall quality. These were trash rags. Adventuresome drivel for young boys, nothing more.

Though the room remained much too dark to see properly, as John ran fingers over the rough, wood-pulp paper, he thought of his father. The great Bernard Covington would have cast the things into the nearest fireplace without second thought. Rags such as these had never been intended for consumption by men such as the Covingtons.

John knew this well. In fact, it was the reason he was smiling. Picking up a small stack, he turned them to catch as much of the distant candlelight as possible. After flipping past a number of *Varney the Vampire* and an incomplete run of *Black Bess*, John stopped. The publication he had been looking for wasn't as old as the rest. The headline had been printed with a bold, whimsical font typically employed by circus posters. Letter by letter, his eyes devoured the title.

Spring-Heeled Jack: The Terror of London

Both above and beneath the title were fanciful illustrations of Londoners in varying states of distress--all of them, recoiling from the titular antagonist. Spring-Heeled Jack, the very specter said to have haunted England's green and pleasant land these past fifty years, appeared in every panel. Skulking around corners, leaping overhead and overall, making a proper menace of himself. The artist had based the appearance of the fiend on eyewitness testimonies-- depicting ole Jack with curved claws, a mouth full of fangs and two horns protruding from his forehead.

Hungrily, John's eyes swept across the central and largest illustration. Below Jack was a horse drawn carriage. The driver, whip in hand, was gaping up at the spring-heeled terror soaring overhead. In the carriage's windows, two faces were drawn, as well as little hands pressed firmly against the glass. Passengers, John remembered, as a slanted grin grew on his lips. After placing the remaining Dreadfuls back into their hiding place, he slid the drawer closed. The Terror of London felt warm upon his lap. An effect that was strangely comforting. Inside, locked within badly penned drivel, adventure was waiting to live again.

The old man rolled up to the desk which had been his for a very long time--whether the portraits of his progenitors liked it or not. After setting down the magazine, he mused at the sudden juxtaposition. Obscuring a patch of hand-worked filigree was a scrap of worthless trash. A publication intended to entertain a class of people who would never know the term Bureau Mazarin.

Straightening his spectacles, John found that his eyes wanted to wander. To regard the strange tableau at his right. The arrangement of blood and bone was abominable--belonging even less than the magazine, but he pushed it from his thinking. Then, with a deep, cleansing breath, John turned the paper cover of *Spring-Heeled Jack: The Terror of London.*

As his eyes scanned the first few paragraphs, memories began to unblur. Out of the haze appeared a small horse drawn carriage led by a heavy-eyed driver. The thing rumbled as it moved down a winding dirt road with rolling moors on one side and a steep drop-off on the other. There was a city nearby, from whence the carriage had come. Canterbury, John recalled. A fact, oddly, never mentioned in the text.

Coming around the bend, the driver (a man called George Plott) caught sight of something that made his eyes go wide. Though he had passed the old church many times before, George was less inclined to do so at night. The thing was more corpse than former house of God. Its roof, as well as the south and eastern walls, were gone completely--returned to rubble and dust at some point in the previous century. Despite this, the structure yet supported a pair of windows and a crooked door frame--features which, in the eyes of George Plott, had always approximated a face. Seeing them now, the man licked his lips and swallowed hard.

The driver's mind worked feverishly while weighing his own threadbare courage. Part of him wanted to snap the reins--to race his horse drawn carriage past the ruin as fast as possible. The other half wanted to turn around and attempt the route again in the morning. As it happened, many seconds passed before he noticed that the moon was missing. In the dark, a panicked George Plott squinted to see, but the world was shrouded. His eyes would adjust, but for now all they could discern was the pale, box-like ruin on the road ahead. Even in the pitch black, the church glared with square, empty eyes.

The sound was sudden--jarring. Shattering the still of perfect night was a sound most terrible. Part cry, part howl, it rang and it soared--gripping the carriage driver's heart as if in the talons of some hellish raptor. If asked whether he were hearing the voice of man or beast, George Plott would not have been able to say.

As if on cue, the moon broke free of its cloud to shine a solitary beam upon the glaring ruin. There on the wall, directly above glassless windows, which now seemed more like screaming mouths than eyes...there stood a man. Or perhaps, not a man. The fiend lunged, belching forth a burst of blue phosphorescence. The display froze poor George Plott where he sat. His joints felt no more supple than those of a marble statue, but the horse was moving plenty. It snorted, angrily shaking its head as if to deny the very existence of the howling thing. The animal's panic was inadvertently forcing the carriage back--nearer and nearer to the edge of the road and the steep drop-off just beyond.

It was then, as he struggled for control of the beast, that George Plott remembered that his carriage held passengers. Emboldened, he pulled hard on one of the reins--desperate to turn his horse the other way round. Behind, the night once again flashed blue. George turned to the church, needing to locate his enemy. But the howling fiend was no longer on the wall--it was in the road.

In the moonlight, a pallid face was visible, as well as a pair of inhuman eyes that burned like balls of cold fire. The fiend was shaped like a man. Tall, gaunt and dressed in a long black cloak over what might have been an oilskin. By God, the thing had horns.

In mid sprint, the creature who could be none other than the fabled Spring-Heeled Jack, leapt high into the air--ten feet, twenty--more!

With the cries of his passengers in his ears, George looked up just in time to see a final crack of blue flame. The world flashed into livid detail, before once again going dark.

GONNNG!

The grandfather clock rang loud and true--filling every nook of the drawing room. John flinched, clutching at his chest. His heart raced--either from the excitement of the story or of the jarring nature of being pulled out of it. Unnoticed, the Dreadful fell from his hands, flopping limply upon the Bureau Mazarin.

GONNNG!

Again the clock thundered and John turned to the south wall. He stared into the darkness, directly upon a face he could not see. He stared like that for a long time as every successive chime was counted by the old man's bones.

Twelve. That was the final number. He had been right after all. The hour had indeed been late.

Once the echoes of the clock's declaration had faded, John turned in his Alderman No. 9. His spine was straighter than before. His ears more acutely aware of the suffocating silence. Extending a shaky hand, he slid the candelabra to the right--fully illuminating the abominable arrangement there. Most of the bones were thin and curved, though some were large enough to have once held eyes. The leavings of Covington Manor's many cats had been easy enough to acquire. The animals had all been so trusting--unable to sense danger until it was too late. A sacrifice both unfortunate and necessary. The book had called for lives. For organs and bones and their connective strings.

Blood had been the final ingredient. The blood of the summoner.

Acutely aware of the space growing between himself and the final stroke of midnight, John leaned forward. Reaching out, he slid the candelabra closer to the grim menagerie--taking care not to disturb the design beneath. The five-pointed star had been difficult to render, what with the special ink being his own blood. Thinking of it, John felt a twinge of pain under the bandages on his left hand. It was a good pain. It meant that none had been harmed for the night's endeavor save for himself and a couple of cats.

With a shaky hand, John opened a pocket watch, then abruptly snapped it shut. Already two minutes past midnight. Had he done something wrong?

John fingered at his collar, finding it difficult to breathe. He thrust a key into the desk's central and most shallow drawer, extracting a small book. Leather-bound and embossed with the image of a five-headed serpent, the book appeared far older than the man who held it. John flipped to an illustration which closely resembled his obscene work of art. The left page showed a detailed illustration of a goat-faced pentagram above a bit of text which read: *"blood of the summoner."* Opposite this was scratched a list of ingredients--instructions on creating the very tableau that now besmirched his great-grandfather's precious desk. John's eyes narrowed, reading each item carefully before falling upon a phrase written below in a far shakier hand.

"He calls at midnight." John whispered the line. His voice sounded so small--so far away. A chill found the nape of his neck, stiffening the tiny white hairs there. John looked up, devouring his surroundings. Though no breeze could have infiltrated his sanctum, the candle-glow danced upon every surface.

Moments later, a new sound boomed into existence. Not the brassy gong of a grandfather clock, but something like the first note of a thunderclap. Hearing this, John's heart galloped, fueled with the thrill of the moment and of moments still to come. Again the thunder boomed--and again and again.

For a brief moment, John worried the sounds would rouse the servants, but of course, such a thing was impossible.

This hellish knocking... It was only for him.

The old man's eyes were firmly fixed upon the massive double doors. He, himself, had locked them hours ago, after Mayhew had taken his uneaten supper away. One second the doors appeared distant, the next they were close enough to touch. With a steadiness that would have surprised him on a different day, John pushed forward a key--closer and closer--toward a tiny hole he could not see.

"Probably best to keep that locked, John. Privacy and all that..."

The voice was winter breeze--a scalpel sliding through air and darkness with deft abandon. As John turned, his body felt stiff. There, in front of the large window, peering out into the moonless night there stood a man. Or perhaps, not a man. Pale, smartly dressed, and skeleton thin.

"It's late, John," said Gideon Crux. "Shouldn't you be in bed?"

The old man tried to answer but his throat was too dry and he nearly choked.

"Mr. Crux," John sputtered at last. "You've come."

"Of course. Refusing a summons would be rude...and there is nothing I detest in this world more than discourtesy. Especially when such *pains* were taken." The thing by the window spoke in tones of polite conversation, but there was a storm brimming just beneath. "I wonder...will begging work half as well if you only use one hand?" A startling sound sliced through the still--like a deep draft taken in through the nose. "That cut smells deep."

"Begging..." Spat the old man. "You'll hear no begging tonight. Not from me."

"Bold words... but ultimately impotent." Gideon Crux turned a shining black eye from the window--setting his gaze upon his host. Then he began to walk around the darkened room, admiring its decor as if for the first time. "Forgive me. I fear the long years in this business have filled me with the blood of a pessimist. Tell me, John--have you the date?"

John sighed, resignedly wheeling himself back to the Bureau Mazarin. "I know what you're thinking...but you are wrong."

"Wrong am I?" Mock-outrage had entered the slithery voice. "Age has emboldened you, John. Though it seems to have done little for your sense of propriety. Wrong, indeed." The voice of Gideon Crux had become playful. "As of three minutes ago, the date is the seventh of August...in the year of your Lord, eighteen hundred and eighty eight. You, John Arthur Covington, latest in a long line of blah-blah-blah...have whiled away all the years in your contract, save five. My presence in this room, at this late hour, can mean but a single thing...you, nearing the end of said contract, wish to renegotiate the terms. It is not exactly a new story."

Scowling, John worked his jaw and said nothing.

"As I said..." continued Gideon Crux. "I have been in this business a very long time. And, if I were being *kind*, I might suggest that you save your mewling words. I have heard them all before and in every imaginable order. The letter of the contract is set--as is that which is owed for services rendered. Even a proper *two-handed* beg would do little to change that."

"I've already told you..." John's voice came out half a whisper. "I didn't call you here to beg. I have no delusions, Mr. Crux. From where I sit, I can see the door at the end of this journey, and I know what lies on the other side. Unfortunately, the thought of another five years--waiting--rotting away in this chair..." Vehemently, John shook his head. "I don't need time, Mr. Crux. What I need is to live. To feel something real--if only for a single night."

The old man in the chair averted his eyes and said nothing more.

"Interesting..." Gideon Crux uttered the word slowly, thoughtfully, as if savoring the unexpected spice. "How very interesting." His voice was distant at first and then, suddenly too loud, too close. *"Tell me John, what exactly would you like to feel? Escape? Release? The earth, once more burning beneath your heels?"*

"Yes." John Covington had to fight off a shudder. "All of that. Dear God, yes." John's words seemed to explode out of him, but they felt weighted. Contorted by something like shame.

"God is not here, John," hissed the knife-like voice of Gideon Crux.

The moments that followed were long. Unbearably long. The only sounds were thoughtful footsteps, traveling from one side of the room to the other, and the incessant ticks of a clock that no longer mattered. Unable to bare the tension, John unlocked another of the desk's seven drawers. From this, he extracted a glass center bowl--lidless and quite empty. Flickering light played within the many hand-cut facets, lending them an eldritch quality.

"Always liked that bowl," mused Gideon Crux. "Though...seeing it again, I can't help but wonder. Which is more empty? The bowl itself? Or the man who is unable to fill it?"

John snickered. "I'd say it were a draw." After a long, silent moment, he set the object down upon the Bureau Mazarin. "This bowl once belonged to my great aunt Helena. It has not held fruit in over ten years. Not since..." His eyes drifted to the Penny Dreadful. To the illustration of the carriage and to the devilish fiend who leapt and soared above. "Since that last trip to the country. On a long, winding road, just outside Canterbury."

"Ah yes," The voice of his guest reflected newfound indifference. "I remember Canterbury. Though, to tell you the truth, John...I much prefer the version described in that penny novel. If only it were life that imitated art and not the other way round, eh?"

"That rag is a fiction. Trite nonsense."

"Oh I know it is, John. I *know*." Crux spoke as if to a wounded child. "That night outside Canterbury was wrought with more of your trickster nonsense and little else. Leaping upon that carriage and slapping the cheeks of its driver. One! Two!" Sounding dejected, Gideon Crux unleashed a long sigh. "At least you scared the hell out of him. I quite doubt the wretch was ever the same again...not to mention *the horse*."

"I didn't scare anyone!" said John, a quiet maelstrom beneath his words. "Not me. Never me. That was Jack."

Gideon Crux gave a shrug. "Your point is a moot one, John. Besides, whatever name you want to use, the real story wasn't exactly the sort of thing that sells books, now is it?"

John Covington glared with a tremble upon his upper lip.

"What the public wants--nay, craves...is tragedy. Excitement. Ghastly piled on top of horrendous!" This, Crux said with a dramatic flourish of one bone-thin arm. "Canterbury may have been a laugh, but as a final act I found it woefully lacking. You had been saving that last jaunt up for over nine years and the best you could come up with was a panicked horse and some rosy cheeks. If you ask me, John...your work peaked where it began."

No response.

"Oh come now... tell me you haven't forgotten the Blacksheath Fair! Ohh, I can picture the two girls as if they were right beside us now. They could not have been more than fourteen. The papers said the assailant was no man, but a horned fiend that, without provocation, did fall upon these poor defenseless moppets. Do correct me, but I recall reading that both blouse and skin had been torn open by iron claws. Shredded, John...the way a lion will a gazelle, before licking off the skin. Sadly, before the fiend could be apprehended, it was said to have leapt a tall fence and bounded away--*all with maniacal laughter on its lips.*"

As he gazed into the facets of the glass center bowl, the old man found himself wishing it would spontaneously shatter. When the voice of Gideon Crux resumed, it came in an ice cold whisper.

"But that isn't the full story, is it John? The papers didn't know about your eyes, but I do. I was right by your side. I remember the wanton passions they held. Say whatever you will. Place the blame upon some alter ego if it helps you stomach another night, but I know the truth. You enjoyed hurting those girls, John. You relished their every shriek and you wanted more. Wanted to go deeper."

"No! That wasn't me! I never wanted to hurt anyone. Not ever!" John slammed a hand down onto hard Mahogany. "God damn you."

"Oh he does, John. Believe me he does. Perhaps you should have called him instead." A short series of steps carried Gideon Crux to the other side of the desk--the flickering flames lending him an aspect of the horrific. "But then, God could never fill your dear Auntie's bowl."

Gideon Crux--everything about the man was too narrow. Prominent bones jutted out above the hollows that were his cheeks. Crowning these were two of the bluest eyes that John had ever seen. They burned and they froze and by God, they did not blink. The man wore no hat, only a crop of pale hair which was slicked back--plastered to his scalp.

As John drank in his guest's countenance, he watched thin, tattered lips part to reveal a row of sliver-like teeth. These had the shimmer of pearls and were far too numerous for a human jaw. The offered expression both approximated and parodied a smile. Seeing it turned John's bowels into ice--forcing him to face the sort of creature he had once again invited into his home.

"'Once more unto the breach, dear friends. Once more. Or close the wall up with our English dead.'" The fierce blue eyes stared and burned and still they did not blink. "'In peace there's nothing so becomes a man as modest stillness and humility. But when the blast of war blows in our ears, then imitate the action of the tiger... Stiffen the sinews, summon up the blood.'" As he spoke, the man-shaped thing stalked around the bend of the desk. The suit he wore was neat, if a handful of decades out of style. Absently, his sharp hand brushed some unseeable dust from an equally sharp shoulder. And when the foot of the Alderman No. 9 had been reached, Gideon Crux stopped to glare. "You pretend to regret. To possess no blame...yet I did not summon myself. Not tonight and not fifty years ago. You can lie to me but not to yourself. Never yourself. I know you, John. You wish to be the tiger. To feel claws sprout from your fingers. Even, for one last time, to leap and soar with the unfettered lusts of Spring-Heeled Jack burning in your chest. Admit it, John. Say it."

"Yes." The old man's voice came low but with an edge.

Long fingers wrapped around the armrests of the rolling chaise as Gideon Crux pushed so close to the old man, that scarcely a centimeter separated their noses. John tried to wheel back, but the added weight of the thin man was incredible. Utterly disproportionate to his slight, bony frame.

"Sorry. Didn't catch that."

"Yes!" Blurted John. "Yes, damn you!"

"Then give me a real ending!"

When the gash that was Crux's mouth opened again, John could almost see his reflection in those tightly packed slivers of pearl.

"No more of this fear-mongering, trickster nonsense. Screaming girls, toppled carriages, and slaps on the cheek might be good for a laugh, but I want a final act worthy of the immortal bard. A misadventure for all time. Deliver me this, John and we shall have betwixt us, an amended accord." With this, Gideon Crux straightened, gliding back a step. Then, he extended a hand.

John had to fight just to hold onto consciousness--his face a mask of determination. Wordlessly, he reached out, seized the creature's hand and shook. Then, pulling away, John set that hand upon the empty center bowl and shoved it forward.

Once again, an unsettling smile stretched the tattered lips of Gideon Crux. He swung a skeleton arm over the bowl. Then, with a flick of the wrist, he dropped numerous *somethings* that pinged, thin and high--bell-like.

"You ask for one final jaunt... I give you five. One for every year I now reclaim."

When John could breathe normally again, he redirected his gaze. The center bowl now held five small berries. They looked like black currants but on closer inspection, John saw that they weren't black at all, but red.

"These are different." He sputtered the words, unable to look away from the red currants that were somehow darker than black. "Crux...why do they look different?"

"Our contract has been altered--per your request, John. I suggest you not squabble over every letter." Gideon Crux smoothed out the lapels of his out of style jacket. "Doing so at this stage would be most...*discourteous*."

Heart pounding near out of his chest, John raised his eyes to the spot where his guest had been standing. Of Gideon Crux, there was no sign, but at the end of the Bureau Mazarin were objects he had never seen before. A rather fashionable top hat and long coat--the garb of a modern English gentleman. In the low light, the garments looked full black, but somehow John knew that was not their true color.

It was all too much. With a weak gasp, the old man slumped deeper into his Alderman No. 9 and allowed consciousness to slip away.

There might have been dreams. Of flying. Of air moving past his face. Of legs that could feel and carry and leap. But if such things did exist, they were obliterated by the clap of bottled thunder, which exploded in John's skull. The sound both jarring and terrible was followed by another, just as loud. And then again. The old man craned his head toward the doors of the drawing room. Someone was knocking.

"Sir?" called a distant voice. "Can you hear me? Are you alright?"

The panicked voice felt familiar. Slowly, the old man stirred, but every inch of him ached. Placing hands on the rails of his rolling chaise, he forced himself into a sitting position. The pain came from everywhere, but dulled quickly. It was then that John realized he had been dreaming. Not of flying, but of darker things. Spells of blood and bone--and of a late night palaver with the devil. It was all perfectly ludicrous.

"Mr. Covington. If you can hear, me, please..."

"I'm here, Mayhew" John cried out at last.

"Sir!" The voice on the other side of the doors flared up with relief. "Thank heavens! We feared--that is... I have been knocking for quite some time."

The old man could hear the relieved voices of further staff alongside the shuffling of feet. His vision proved slow to focus, but John could see the candelabra. The candles it had once held now existed only as pools of hardened wax besmirching the surface of his great grandfather's precious desk.

"I'm fine, Mayhew. Just...fell asleep in the memoirs again."

"Ah, the old memoirs," said Mayhew "Another ink well drained, I presume?"

"You know me too well." As John said this, a flash of pain kicked hard, causing his teeth to grind. When he opened his eyes again, they focused on something which laid upon the desk. Though he could not recall how it might have happened, the magazine had been torn utterly in two. As if by themselves, the old man's eyes flitted across an intact section of title.

--*Jack: The Terror of London*

"Well done, Sir." There came a pause. "Will you be taking your breakfast there in the drawing room?"

"No!" The word exploded past John's lips before he had thought to stop it. His eyes thrust forth like daggers. They were focused on what lay past the torn magazine and hardened pools of wax. Unlike the old Dreadful, the occultist tableau was quite untouched. "I believe that today, I shall breakfast in the parlor."

"Very good, Sir," chimed Mayhew--newfound mirth in his voice.

As footsteps padded away, John's eyes moved to the glass center bowl. As he stared, the heels of his dead feet began to throb hotly--pounding in time with his tired heart. Inside the bowl were what looked like small, dark berries. He counted them once and then again. Four. Why were there only four?

As if in a dream, John's head turned. Slowly, the Bombay table which held his guilty pleasures came into view. Strewn atop the rich wooden surface sat a stylish top hat and coat. By the look of things, they had been tossed there rather unceremoniously. Beneath these, poking out by only a few inches, was something which glinted in the morning sun. Something silver and very, very sharp. Seeing the tip of the knife had a profound effect on the man in the chair. And in that moment, John Arthur Covington remembered every detail of his dream. His ghastly, wonderful dream.

In retrospect, he had gotten his wish. The one thing he had yearned for ever since Canterbury. John had once more felt the earth burning beneath his heels. The red currant had twisted him into an entirely new terror for Londontown. One which had stalked cobbled streets and around dark alleys-- not with mischief in his heart, but with the cold power of a scalpel. The adventure had been a messy one, but such was to be expected.

A surgeon's work is nothing if not bloody.

Letter to Evalene

Letter To Evelene

The wounded man pulled hard but the massive hinges were thick with rust and rigor mortis.

If he had been able, Roman would have kicked the door right then. Instead, he renewed his grip and pulled harder. Finally, the hinges uttered a metallic squeak and relented, sending Roman back on his ass. What came next was an ear-clapping bang, but if this was the door slamming down or the atom bomb that had just gone off in his leg, Roman wasn't sure.

As he lay on his back, awash with throbs of white-hot pain, the thought of getting up seemed ridiculous. Right then, more than anything, Roman Santiago just wanted to be done. To give in and let the unceremonious end to his story have its way with him. Problem was, there was still too damn much on his chest. So, with a great bellow he managed to reach a skewed half-crouch position.

Taking a few moments to recover from the effort, Roman glared down at the rusted old hinges which had almost defeated him. They were screwed into a large slab of wood. A trap door which now lay flush against the floor of the old attic.

Trap door. The door to a trap. Roman thought with a smirk. *Pretty fucking apt.*

Standing up brought tears to his eyes. He had to force himself to reach for a handmade looking latch. With a grunt, he slid it over the edge of the door. The thing didn't look very strong, but it didn't have to hold forever. Just long enough.

Roman looked around, wondered again about the boy.

"This was your room, wasn't it?" He asked the darkness, though it did not reply. "I dunno... must have been kinda cool. Just you and your stuff. Away from all the bullshit downstairs."

Suddenly, Roman teetered then proceeded to swear at his stupid leg. Not only had the wound had not improved, the skin had become hot to the touch and seemed to be banging out a rhythm. It was a hard hitting rock beat currently stabbing at the backs of both eyes. A beat that sounded an awful lot like the bassline of an old Van Halen song. Snickering at the absurdity of his own brain, Roman reached for the rifle he had found, then shoved the buttstock under one armpit. Leaning on the weapon brought forth a wave of relief.

Using the rifle as a crutch, Roman hobbled over to the far side of the room. Every step hurt, but served to bring him closer to his final stop. The end of the line was a small wooden desk. The kind with compartments, drawers and a child-sized chair tucked underneath.

"Hope you don't mind, kid." Roman sat down, propping the rifle against the wall and clenching his teeth from the pain. "See, I'm fresh out of supplies."

The desk was dusty, but in fair enough order. On the left was a ceramic cup--bright red and crafted with all the artisan passion of a kid forced to make pottery in art class. Luckily, the thing's function won out over its form. In its clutches was a number of pens and pencils. Sifting through the arsenal, Roman slid out a mechanical pencil and clicked it twice.

Figurative sword in hand, he began opening and closing drawers. The third one held a spiral bound notebook with a name written on the cover in blue marker.

PROPERTY of EDWARD JACOB DEVONS

Reading this caused a pang of real sadness to rise in the man, but he shook it off. Nearly a third of the pages were filled with sketches--all of them birds.

There were between two and four per page--each with the name of the species beside a corresponding date.

"Hey," Said Roman, genuinely impressed. "These are good. You got some real talent here, kid."

Granted, to the man's eyes, all the drawings just looked like birds, but he recognized the pointy head of the cardinal when he came to it. Some had been colored while others were rendered only in the shiny grey of a No. 2 pencil. On the last of the used pages was an especially large and detailed sketch. Roman recognized that one too--it was an owl. Beside it stood the handwritten caption. 'Barred Owl: Date seen:______'

The man stared at that empty line right up until a sliding, slumping sound from below pulled him back to the moment. Setting the notebook down, he ran a palm over the page. Then, after clicking the eraser end one more time, he began to do the one thing he had ever been any good at. Roman Santiago began to write.

Dearest Evelene,

I know what happened between us was my fault. I just hope you can find a way to forgive your dumb old Roman. It's already been a few days since you left. Feels like years. I wanted to write you one last time because, since we parted, so much of what I did was because of you.

I found the house by chance, just as the sun was going down. For a while I had become aware that I was walking on a path through those woods, though I never would have dared hope for what lay at the end. The house didn't seem to fit into any specific style. It was brown with brown trim--like a big, featureless box. The side facing me was flat with a small awning above the front door--the kind that comes to a peak with shingles on top. Besides this, the only other feature was a small window on what I judged to be a third story. Right from the start, I didn't like the look of that window. It made the house look like it had been shot, right in the head.

The yard was maybe half an acre and full of overgrown grass that had gone to flower. I could see a stone fire pit off to one side, as well as a dirt lot at the end of the path I was on. Parked there were precisely one and one half vehicles.

The old pickup was covered in so much mud I could barely tell the make or model. All four tires were flat but the windows were intact. Next to this, up on four cinder blocks was an old Camaro. Not sure of the year--you were always better at that stuff. Late 60s would be my guess. The hood had been propped open, but judging on the thickness of the spider webs between it and the chassis, I doubt if anyone had looked the old girl's way in a long time.

When I got closer to the house, I could see the left side of that awning was damaged. It looked like it'd been smashed by the fall of a heavy branch. I thought this was kinda strange though, since the closest trees were about fifty feet back. I tried the handle of the front door but, as you'd expect, it was locked. I thought about trying to break the thing down but even if I wasn't about to pass out from the throbbing pain in my leg, I knew a busted front door wasn't going to do me any good later on. So, I decided to have a look around.

The house's east side was where they had put all the rest of the windows and there was no question as to why. Rolling hills, leaves that blazed in a thousand hues of gold and green. It was quite a view. Honest to God, Evelene I wish you could have seen it.

I guess it was then I finally realized where I was. This unnumbered house in the middle of nowhere, a yard surrounded by dense woods, dirt driveway with no mailbox. In more ways than one, I had stumbled upon the proverbial end of the road--number 99 Dead End Drive. At least, that's what I might have called it if all this were one of my shitty books.

Continuing around the east side, I passed a big picture window that looked in on a living room. I could see some bookshelves, an end table and an old tube tv... but it was that couch that really caught my eye. I knew there had to be a way inside--a back door or a bulkhead into a basement. I remember checking the sky then and finding it dimmer than I prefer. Suddenly nervous, I headed straight for the house's back entrance. This door was as locked as the other, but there was a single window just beside.

As I mentioned, the idea of punching any permanent holes in this potential sanctuary made my stomach sink, but I was running short on both time and options. Glass went everywhere but I was careful. I had wrapped the rock in my jacket. Getting through wasn't a ton of fun, but after a few tense and wholly graceless minutes, I fell on my ass inside of ole 99--the last house on Dead End Drive.

Since part of me was waiting for some bearded redneck to step out of the shadows and blow my head off, I proceeded quietly. Moving from kitchen to hallway to foyer. Out of stupid habit I flicked a light switch, yielding predictable results. The place smelled ancient. Like dust and old cigarette smoke with a hint of squirrel crap thrown in.

Around a corner I came to that grand oasis I had glimpsed from outside. The living room wasn't much to look at, but it felt like Shangri La. To be honest, I don't even remember hitting that old threadbare couch. I guess you could say my body went exactly as far as it needed to before throwing some master kill switch.

During that first night, I woke up only once and it was in a cold sweat.

I remember being afraid. Looking from shadow to shadow, wondering what kind of idiot would have passed out before thoroughly checking out his surroundings. Even if there was no one else squatting in the house, there was the matter of the open hole I'd left on the north side. Hell, the least I could have done was find a weapon or turn the couch around so it wasn't facing those huge windows. Of course, I probably don't have to tell you what kind of dumb-ass you married, Evelene. I know I don't. But this was survival 101 level shit.

Anyway... it wasn't long before I heard it. The thing that surely had woken me in the first place. I swear to God, that sound made my blood freeze. The repeating tone was familiar but difficult to place. Shit, I hadn't heard it since I was maybe nine years old. Those summers on my grandparents farm, up in El Paso.

It was an owl. Just a damn owl, calling out to the malevolent dark.

I meant to get up then, to do something about that open window but... I heard it again. Four notes--once and then repeated. The fourth and last were a little higher and louder than the rest. A simple question.

Who looks for you?

That's what Grammy-Nan once told me they were saying, the owls. When my eyes opened again, it was morning. Just after 9 according to my wristwatch. I couldn't believe it--I had slept all night. Not up a tree or under some rusty old combine but on a real live couch. Right then I could have turned over and gone right back to sleep for another day or two. If only, that is, I hadn't used up all my stupid pills the night before.

I tried the kitchen faucet and after some violent sputtering, a steady stream of what looked like weak tea came rushing out. The stove didn't work but remembering the fire pit outside, I started opening cabinets. Most were full of empty boxes and the aforementioned squirrel crap, but the lower ones had a few good pots. I decided to let the faucet run for a minute while I went to check out the front door. Unfortunately, it'd been fixed with a pretty sturdy looking padlock. Without the key, that thing was going nowhere fast. Just like yours truly.

Back in the kitchen, the water had gone from weak tea to what I would categorize as *very weak tea*. Figuring that was about as good as I was going to get, I filled up three pots worth. The water would need boiling first, but I reckoned it was better than what I might find in the toilets.

None of the drawers held anything I could start a fire with, but I managed to find a flashlight. It was one of those big silver Maglites, too. The kind you used to say could double as a gladiator weapon. Small miracle, the batteries still had some juice, but that was pretty much all the kitchen had to offer.

On that first floor, there were still two doors I hadn't tried. The first ended up being a bathroom. Under the sink were some basic first aid supplies which was a whole other kind of relief. I knew I couldn't put off looking at my leg for much longer, but my stomach was screaming too loud for that to come first. The second door opened to a staircase leading down. Bravely, I brandished my new gladiator weapon and headed on down. The basement was pretty much what you'd expect. At the bottom of the stairs was a rusty old washer/dryer combo and numerous baskets of laundry. They looked like a gathering of hapless disciples ready to plunge headlong into the top loading mouth of their volcano God.

Directly to my right was yet another door with a handmade sign hanging above it. This read "The Matt Cave".

Expecting the door to be locked, I was pleasantly surprised when it swung open. Inside, I learned the place was less an actual cave and more of a survivalist's wet dream. This was a fully stocked, state of the art bug-out bunker--complete with one cot, one recliner, wide screen tv and of course, the obligatory Confederate flag on the wall. Opposite this was a framework of wooden shelves that had been stocked with just about anything one might need to survive.

In case of apocalypse, break glass.

One section was dedicated to boxes containing small brown packages--flat and rectangular with MRE printed in bold black letters. I grabbed the one labeled *beef patty* and tore it open. I had never actually tried one of these Meal Ready to Eats before, and I guess my stomach was hoping for a perfect beef patty just staring up and waiting to be devoured. Instead, there were a bunch of smaller packages. These were covered in far more instructions than I had patience to read, but I was able to discern two things. One--water was required to cook the patty inside its pouch. And two--one of the packages contained cheese filled crackers! I swear to God, Evelene, I ate those crackers so damn fast, I'm lucky I still got fingers enough to write. The pouch marked *cheese spread with bacon* was next. I knew it was for the beef patty, but hunger wins out over pride every time. After sucking out every drop of that non-dairy cheese food, I turned the packet inside-out and licked it clean.

Scanning the shelves, I found boxes of ammunition, several kinds of batteries and maybe a dozen cases of toilet paper... yet for some insane reason, this Matt guy, in all his doom-prepping, red-neck wisdom, neglected to purchase himself an ample supply of bottled water--or any for that matter. So, grabbing a box of matches I headed back upstairs to continue with my original plan.

It took me three trips but I hauled all the pots outside, water and all. This time I used the back door, which was secured only by a simple deadlock that unlatched easily from inside. The fire pit was pretty big--flat on top with plenty of surface area. Facing the thing were two lounging type lawn chairs. One was on its side, half obscured by the tall grass.

I could see some strange, blackened sticks in the bottom of the pit. They were partly buried by mounds of blackened ash and soot. I knew none of that would catch, but next to the chairs there was a box with some dry kindling, and almost six cords of chopped wood.

Starting the fire wasn't hard and pretty soon I had it roaring and crackling and looking alright. Carefully I placed the pots directly on the flames--praying they weren't going to melt or something. At that point I plopped down into the closest lounger, leaned back and just drifted off. For a second there, everything seemed to melt away, two years of running, you leaving me--all of it. I had water boiling, cheese food in my belly and the morning sun. Hell, for almost a full minute there, I even forgot about my stupid Goddamn leg.

Truth was, I hadn't looked at it in a couple of days. There had been no way to clean the wound anyhow. But that was then. That was out there. This unlikely house in the woods had changed everything.

A sharp hiss pulled my attention back to the fire. The pots hadn't melted but they were bubbling and boiling. Using my sleeve as an oven mitt, I pulled each one out and set them on the ground. After that I must have sat in that chair for over an hour, just thinking and waiting for the water to get cool enough to drink. This place, this house at the end of the road... it seemed an awful lot like a haven. A sanctuary in a world that had forgotten the definition of the word.

Eventually, I had that drink I'd been dying for all morning. It tasted like dirt but knowing I wasn't going to die of dysentery, helped a lot. I poured a bit into the last two pouches of the MRE and after forcing down some old fashion heatless cooking, I decided I had sat long enough.

For a minute, I just stood there, staring into the flames--soaking up as much warmth as I could. Then, just before I turned away, a piece of charred wood crumbled and fell, sending up a great puff of ash. That was when I noticed the sticks I had seen earlier. Black as before but otherwise unburnt-- they were strange as sticks went. Curved and completely smooth as if only the bark had been charred away. To be honest, the longer I looked, the more they looked like bones... but I didn't want to think about that.

I knew they would catch up with me soon. Don't have to tell you, Darling--no matter how far we ran, they were never far behind. But... I was getting myself all worked up again. You were always my rock Evelene. Always. I'm not trying to throw any guilt around, neither. Just stating a fact.

Back inside the house, I spent the better part of forty minutes pushing an olive green refrigerator in front of a broken window. And at the end, my leg was throbbing loud enough for the neighbors to hear. That was it--I knew I had to get on with the one thing I had already put off for too long. I tell you darling, taking down my pants has never been less fun. The wound was swollen and even less pretty than I'd imagined it'd be. And it smelled.

It happened about a week after you'd left, but right then the whole thing replayed in my mind. The running, the falling directly on that tree branch--how I had to break it off before I could pull it out. Thing is, that story doesn't matter. Doesn't really have a point. This one does. I want you to know what I did here. I want you to be proud.

In all, it took almost an hour to get all the remaining pieces of wood out, but in the end my leg was clean and dressed. The pain was still pretty bad, though duller than it had been.

After that, my lame self limped through the house. Passing the staircase in the foyer, I looked up--tried to glean some aspect of the second floor. I needed to see what was up there, but I didn't have it in me--not then. I knew I was teetering on the edge of a precipice called delirium. Hell, it was just about all I could do to get back to the couch. I'd have a nap. Just an hour or two.

I hit that couch with the force of a wrecking ball and drifted off to the bassline my leg was pounding out. It was so loud, so steady. All I could think of was that old Van Halen song, Running With The Devil. Back in high school, your brother played that one over and over. Even as I write this, the opening line keeps repeating in my brain.

Always hated that damn song.

By the time I finally woke up, it was raining and it was dark. I checked my watch, 11:01 pm. I had done it again, fallen victim of the magic couch. I got off my ass--suddenly determined to find something I could swing. That's when I remembered the Maglite. Limping back to the kitchen was less fun in the pitch black. Like the night before, my eyes kept trying to decide whether the shadows were really shifting or not. The house had become so dark--so perfectly silent, I thought I might go insane.

Who looks for yooouuu?

I nearly jumped out of my skin when I heard that damn bird again.

As I stood in the dark, trying not to have a heart attack, a funny thing happened. That voice started to sound less like a bird and more like a person. *Who looks for yooouuu?* It was high like the voice of a woman... or a little boy.

I felt a little better when my fingers curled around the flashlight. With that heavy rod of metal destruction in my hand, I felt better. Not loads but, still. Wasting no time, I clicked the button which instantly shot forth a perfect beam of not just light but *sight*.

Who looks for yooouuu? Asked the voice again.

No doubt about it--that was no bird. Suddenly I felt a burning need to see what was making that sound. I looked at the front door--at the gigantic padlock. Who the hell puts one of those on the inside of a front door anyway? I knew the living room looked out onto the wrong side, but I remembered the tiny window I had seen as I first walked up the drive. The one that looked like a bullet hole in the head of this place. Armed with this knowledge and my flashlight cudgel, I decided it was time to go upstairs.

Every step, every board produced a new creak--a new reason to abandon the course and jump back into the warm embrace of that magic couch. It was the question that kept me going. The one coming from the front lawn. Reaching the second floor, I pointed that light in every dark corner that came my way.

I found myself in a narrow hallway. There were two doors and a ladder at the end, presumably leading to the third floor. The rain was louder up there. It helped. Gave me something to focus on. Another few steps brought me to the edge of the first door. Ever so carefully, I peeked inside, scanning every surface with my trusty beam of light. It was a bedroom. Nothing special. Barely big enough for the king size bed and the two dressers. There was laundry on the floor and two windows which continued to flash and bang in time with the storm outside.

The ladder was rickety but it held. After about five steps my head poked through the trap door and into an old attic. I could see a weird wall next to my head, which I later realized was the back of a bookcase. Once fully inside, I could see the room was long and dark. And for what might have been minutes, I forgot all about the flashlight. Thinking on it now, I was fully mesmerized by something at the far end of the room. A tiny glowing rectangle. The window, flashing like it was, had become the sole object in this lifeless universe.

I moved like a sleepwalker. Oblivious to all but that window and the oppressive racket of the rain above. A breeze was my first indication that the glass had been previously broken. When I reached it, I shone a beam of light down, but the floor was clean. When I stuck my head out, I could see that caved-in awning above the front door. That's when I started stringing together a narrative. The awning hadn't been damaged by a falling branch. Someone, it seemed, had taken a swan dive out of this third floor window.

Who looks for yooooouuu?

Fully back in the moment, I peered through the rain--straining to see something, anything. Then a bolt of lightning lit up the world. There was a kid out there--a boy. He was facing the woods. His pale little hands cupped around his mouth.

Who looks for yooouuu? He called out into the malevolent dark.

Rain was blowing in through the window--dripping sweat and dirt into my eyes, but I stared as hard as I could. At the boy but also at the woods. That's when I saw them, Evelene. There were things between those trees. Shadows with eyes and teeth. I wanted to shout, to scream at the kid! Tell him to get the hell out of there! Christ, couldn't he see them?

Who looks for yooouuu?

I couldn't take it. I had to reach that kid and get him inside. Remembering my weapon, I swung a beam of pure light at the trap door. But as I did this, my eyes caught sight of something. Something in the pitch dark blur of my periphery.

In the air, just off to my right, hung two withered things that looked a lot like feet. These swayed and seemed to pivot on some unseen axis. Trembling, unable to breathe, the beam of my light began to move upwards--past ankles, knees, waist. My hands trembled bad, but I couldn't stop or turn or even scream as the specter rotated slowly in mid-air to face me. That night, my dearest darling... the last thing I saw was a horrible sunken face. A mummy's face--all teeth and shadow and rot. It was a sight that left me stabbed and gutted and, apparently, unable to remain upright.

As I fell to the floor, the last thing I remember hearing was the distant voice of a boy calling out in the rain.

Next morning, the only thing that hurt more than my leg was my head. Over my skin blew a cool breeze and I could hear a gentle creaking sound that kept repeating itself. When my vision finally managed to focus, I immediately wished it hadn't. Above and to the right, was the suspended body of a woman. She had long brown hair and was dressed in a pinkish sundress. No shoes though. No eyes neither. Just two empty caverns. God knows how long she had been hanging there--just twisting round on that old rope.

Feeling sick, I scrambled back and up--rushed to the window for air. As daylight had once again claimed the world, the things between the trees were gone. Them and that crazy kid. Right then my gut was hollering to get the Sam Hell out of Dodge, but could I? Discounting the dead lady in the attic, *they* had found me. The same bastards that have been on our heels for two years. Besides, I knew was never gonna make it back on the road. Not with my leg like it was.

So I took in the room--careful to point my eyes at anything but my new friend. Too shook to wonder about the who or the why, I resolved to learn all I could about the what. The setting of the unfortunate woman's story. This wasn't just an attic--it was a bedroom. There were two bookcases, a twin bed and a small writing desk. On the bed--on top of a neatly made comforter, I could see two very contradictory items. First was a package, wrapped neatly in newspaper and topped with a card. Beside this was a rifle--the barrel of which protruded from the bed a good half foot or more. Picking it up, I could sense an immediate change in my mood. Here was a real weapon. A measure of security matched only by the trusty light of day.

Despite how good it felt to hold that gun, my eyes drifted over to the card. To the two words that had been written there: *"My Ward"*. Right then I wasn't sure what to make of that. All I knew is that I felt... I guess *haunted* is the word. For almost an hour, I sat on the bed, staring at that card, just wondering what I was supposed to do next.

You know I've always had a tendency to complain about things. If the going got tough, old Roman was apt to bitch about it. That said, I hope you can believe when I say that what happened next was the most difficult thing I have ever had to do. It took many hours and a good slice of my soul to get through. Truly, I have no desire to detail any of it here. Suffice it to say, the woman in the sundress is now at rest.

Of my time outside that day, I will say this. When I was through, I inspected the spot where that boy had been standing the night before. Funny thing was, despite the ground being all slick and soft from the storm, the only tracks out there were the ones I was leaving.

Back inside, I melted into the magic couch. My eyes fixed on the present and card. I had brought them down earlier but still hadn't decided what I was going to do. "My Ward"--I probably read that a hundred times. I started picking the card up and putting it back down. Did that for a while too. As my fingers carefully slipped out the top triangle of paper, I could feel an energy escaping that dusty old envelope. What I was doing felt morally wrong, but also, somehow, necessary. The front showed a picture of a rocket ship zooming around a planet whose Pangean continents happened to form a large number 9. Inside were the preprinted words: *"This year, have a birthday that's OUT OF THIS WORLD!"*

Underneath that old chestnut was the following message.

To my (not so) little Ward,

I hear that every good bird watcher needs one of these!

PS- The Whistle Stop didn't have a card for a 9 year old with an owl, or any kind of bird for that matter. Obviously we won't be shopping there anymore. Ha! Ha! Oh well, rockets fly too!

XOXO

Love
Mom and Matt

The words seemed to hum in my brain. For a while longer, I just sat there, staring into space. My thoughts turned to the woman I had just put in the ground. *Mom.* I wanted to stop, but my hands were moving by themselves. I picked up the present. Then began to slowly tear away the newspaper. When I saw what was inside, I couldn't stop the shiver from going up my spine. The book was titled 'Owls of North America'.

Only got off that couch once more after that. Just a quick trip to the Matt Cave for some more MRE and a box of shells. After sucking down three packets of bacon flavored cheese spread, I sat my ass back down and I waited. The owl book helped a little but by 10:59 pm, I was ready to crack. There were so many crazy thoughts and theories rolling around my head, I could barely remembered my own name. Then I heard it. The very sound I'd been waiting for.

Who looks for yooouuu? Called the boy on the lawn.

Hearing that kicked my heart into a strange rhythm, fast but irregular--a speed metal waltz. I grabbed the book and the rifle and I headed for the back door. Outside, the night was clear, but my arms and legs felt heavy--atrophied. Just being outdoors without the sun overhead put a fester in my gut. I had to force myself to take every step. Still, somehow I knew I was doing the right thing. Definitely not the smart thing, but the right one.

You spent half your life helping kids, Evelene--half your damn life. All while I tapped away at a keyboard and made shit up. I don't know why we worked for so long, but boil us down to our core components and those are the facts. Do you remember how many kids got out of really bad situations because of you? Forty-one. You probably never knew I kept track but the number is right. Forty-one kids, Evelene. I figured if this really was the dead end of the road, the least I could do was help this one.

I rounded left and then again to turn upon the front lawn. Breathing had become difficult--like rolling-a-boulder-up-a-hill difficult. Good thing my feet remembered what they were there for. Eventually I could see the cars in the drive and the fire pit and past them... I could see the boy. It was all so Goddamned surreal. The closer I got, the more the kid looked flat. Like he was a cardboard cut-out, automatically rotating to prevent me from seeing his face.

"Hey there." I spoke as loud and steady as I was able. "Ward? Is that your name? Ward?"

The boy didn't answer. Instead he simply lifted his hands, cupped them around his mouth and called out his question to the malevolent dark.

"Hey," God, my voice sounded so stupid right then, "I found these... in your room. I think your mom wanted you to have them." I set the book and card down on the ground. But as I moved so did he, making sure his back faced me at all times. It was then I realized that I had moved so far over in attempting to see his face that I was as close to the tree-line as he was. With wide eyes I stole a glance into the darkness to my right. And not twenty feet away, I could see them. Those damned things were practically in a frenzy, yet not a single one seemed willing to venture a single step towards us. Slowly my head turned back to the boy. "That is your room up there, right? The third floor? It's pretty cool up there. I like your... books."

The boy lifted his hands as if I wasn't there. *Who looks for yooouuu?* He cried in the haunting tongue of the owls.

My plan wasn't working. I could see that just as plainly as I could see that the boy called Ward hadn't been alive in some time.

I began to back away. Then I ran for all I was worth. With every step, my leg felt like someone was striking the bone inside with a hammer but I didn't slow until I was through that back door and back on my magic couch. My face felt hot, like I had just stepped inside from the dead of winter. I lay down, refusing to let go of the rifle--not that it was going to do a lick of good anyhow. I knew I had to get a handle on my breathing, but in my mind, all I could see were nightmares. A woman with no eyes, a dead boy and shadows between the trees with eyes like whole cherries.

There was a grinding in my head that I realized was my back molars. Part of me wanted to go back outside--to march right past the boy and into those woods. It wouldn't be clean but at least I wouldn't have to hear that damned question anymore.

Who looks for yooouuu?

I grabbed one of the cushions and slammed it down over my head, pushing my face as far into the couch as it would go. And that brings me to the part in my story I have been dreading most. I don't know if what happened was a dream or some psychic echo--I just know that for the purposes of my own sanity, I have to get it out, Evelene. I can only pray that once you've read this, you won't think less of your Roman.

The vision began with me--only I wasn't me.

There was a woman. We were kissing, but it was more than just kissing. I was pawing her, grinding our bodies together hard enough to leave bruises. In the dream, I glanced over to see a boy standing in the foyer. He was watching. The sight caused an instantaneous change in me--only, I swear to God Evelene, it wasn't me. I jumped up, causing the woman to crash onto the floor. Then I stormed over to the kid.

"What are you, stupid?" Shouted the man/Matt/me.

"I... I was just..."

"You were just what? Just being a little pervert?!" Suddenly, I felt my hand grab the kid and march him to the front door. Somehow I knew it wasn't locked so I threw it open and pushed the boy outside.

"Not tonight Matt." The woman was pleading.

"Hell yes, *tonight*." I spat back, slamming the door then turning a very small key in a very big lock.

"But..." The woman went on, close to tears but not close enough. "They said on the radio it's supposed to get to single digits--did he have his jacket?"

"Damn it Dwynna, he'll be fine. Anyway, the little weirdo fucking likes it out there--with his birds and shit. Hell, maybe tonight he'll spot himself that fucking owl. Hasn't shut up about it for weeks, for Christ sake. Now come on..." I heard my voice soften--adopt a musical quality. "You don't want to go fucking up happy hour, now do you?"

Gazing outside, the woman drew the back of one arm across her face. Then she turned to look at me and though I saw real loathing there, she slowly shook her head and acquiesced.

Just like that, the vision or dream was over. I sat up like I was spring-loaded--glad to be in my own skin. Hearing the ghost boy's question right then was like a kick to the gut, but I finally understood. Maybe not all of it, but enough. I picked up the rifle, limped my ass into that foyer, aimed and squeezed the trigger.

That big Goddamned padlock exploded like two halves of a grenade--leaving a fair sized hole into the door. My hands were my own once more, I reached out for the knob and threw the door open. I could see him, Evelene. The boy was just standing there--in the same place as before. And yeah, those things were there too. Boiling like darkness between the trees. As I moved, my jaws felt rusted... so I pried them the hell open.

"Hey boy!" I shouted in my best impression of a man who I was pretty sure had never once called this kid by his Christian name. A man whom I had so briefly become and now had to again. "Get your ass inside before you freeze to death."

Just like that, Ward put his hands down. Then, ever so slowly, he turned around.

"That's right!" I waved. "You come inside right now. The owls must all be somewhere else tonight."

I saw his face, Evelene. His eyes--they contained the sort of weariness a kid should never know. As the dead boy trudged past, I tried to make eye contact, but he wouldn't look up. And if he had, I wonder... would it have been me he saw standing in that doorway? Or that mean doom-prepping son of a bitch who'd hurt him and treated his mom like she was dog shit?

Today, as I sat, waiting for the eleventh hour on my magic couch, I had a lot of time to think. To let my imagination fill in some gaps that had been left empty for too damn long around here. The woman, Dwynna--I think she snapped. After Ward was gone, I think she pulled the rifle on old Mr. Happy Hour and forced him out the third floor window. Now I'm sure those were bones I saw in that fire pit. Of course, even if Dwynna did avenge her little boy... there must have been nothing left for her. Nothing I reckon, but some rope and a whole lot of oblivion.

Anyway... I watched the sad little ghost boy trudge on--across the foyer and up those stairs.

After he was inside, I didn't bother trying to secure the door--no point in that. Them things had chased us for so long--there was no stopping them now. Just before the boy turned the corner on the second floor, I could hear a swell of excitement from outside. I didn't look though. I just went upstairs.

With this leg of mine, it took way too long to get back to the attic, but here I am. At the end. I'm glad I was able to buy time enough to finish this letter. I just needed you to know, Evelene. So you'd know that I managed to actually do something real. To help this one kid get some rest.

Gotta say, I was kind of hoping he'd be up here. Would have liked to talk to Edward Jacob--to thank him for the way out. Hell, I never would have had the courage otherwise. I know that now. Thing is, ever since you left, Evelene,

I've been having bad thoughts. Things like how I'd rather be dead than go on another worthless fucking day without you--shit like that. Anyway, we'll be together again soon. I know because I can hear them. They're in the house now. See, I had a funny feeling it was the boy keeping those bastards away-- ever since I went out there with his birthday present.

Kinda funny when you think about it. An entire hoard of vampires afraid of one little ghost kid? Sounds like the plot to one of my shitty books.

Love you past forever.

~R

Saltwater Tears

Poor Molly Maeve, she lives between the waves
Waiting for a little one, close enough to keep
Sweet Molly Maeve, she'll take you to her cave
And smother you with kisses, as salty as the deep

The liquid dark flowed around the pale woman. Something was pulling her down, under, beneath. Farther and farther from the world of light. She should have been cold, should have been afraid, but Brona Sheridan was no longer thinking of herself.

You passed this way. Didn't you, darling? She thought this distantly, matter of factly, the way one regurgitates directions for a stranger. Down that road there and left at the Oistigan place, she might as well have said.

Initially, the darkness appeared without form or feature but after a time, shapes began to emerge. As her eyes adjusted, they could by degrees, make out indications--lines and surfaces barely there, yet rapidly becoming more and more real. She became aware of a subtle greenish glow. The farther down she drifted, the brighter it became, until her bare feet were cast in stark silhouette. The weird light seemed a living thing. She watched as it flowed eel-like, extruding itself from an undersea cave. And in that moment, Brona Sheridan was filled with an undeniable sense of purpose. It felt a little like recalling something unfinished. A stew left burning on the stove, or forgotten laundry, left to dry in the rain. Her eyes flashed greenly. The cave's mouth was fringed with rocky outcroppings that brought to mind jagged witch-teeth and suddenly Brona felt as if she were about to be gobbled up. By now, the light had wormed its way into her brain, and just as she thought she could bare it no longer, the woman heard a voice. It was a small thing, barely there. It drifted along the eel-glow from deep inside the cave, whispering a single heart-shattering word.

"Mama?"

With a jolt, the pale woman opened her eyes. She was out of breath but back on land. Back home. Safe and slumped in her husband's favorite chair. Only there

Beside her, the hearth-fire burned. She had not been asleep for long, or so the logs told her. What moisture remained inside them, cracked and popped above a gentle roar. She could not precisely recall her dream, only the bitter echoes of some forgotten purpose. Something she had meant to finish. With a shudder, Brona squeezed tighter the soft object in her arms, trying in vain to remember what had slipped away. Then, from outside came the heavy falls of familiar boots. It was a sound which, under normal circumstances, would have seemed like the music of angels.

The front door was old. Solid oak and notched from use. It swung open slowly and not without protest from the hinges, which were in all likelihood, older still. Brona turned to the man in the doorway. For a moment, the soft parts around her eyes flushed with heat though her body, it seemed, could spare no more tears.

"John." She said her husband's name. Only this. Tomorrow she would have the energy to greet him properly, but for now she hoped beyond all reason, that the name would be enough.

"Brona?" The man made a question of the name. Then stepped inside the cottage and swung shut the heavy door.

John Sheridan was a tall, broad-chested brute. Bearded and sunburnt, but with sapphire eyes that had no choice but to sparkle at all times. They were eyes that Brona had always adored. Eyes that on certain rare occasions, had turned her bones into butterflies. And yet now those eyes contained only fear. The man's bear-paw hand, moved to unfasten a single button on his jacket. The weathered garment was tossed blindly, falling just short of a brass hook to drop into a damp heap on the floor.

"I'm back, darling." He said at last. "I came straight home from port. Tomorrow is Sunday. I meant to bring home a nice squab for dinner, I did. But before I made it to Jacob's, I was stopped in the street by two men. Eamos Walsh and Alroy Mchodge. They had been waiting for me, you see." John paused then, just for a beat. "Old Hodge... he was the one that did the talking. Oh God, Brona. The things he told me." His voice had picked up a tremble. "I need you to tell me they aren't true."

At this, the pale woman shifted in her chair, turning back to the hearth. Unwilling to accept the offered silence, John crossed the room in three great strides to kneel beside his wife. He reached out a hand to touch her arm, but stopped. How pale and thin that arm had become.

"Brona, please." John's voice hitched. "Talk to me! What happened? How is my little girl? Ena, is she going to be alright?"

The eyes of John Sheridan, usually so tender and kind, now searched the face of his wife for some indication of response. When none came, he stood and took a step towards the opposite corner of the small cottage. In the semi-darkness was a door that seemed too small to permit a man of his frame. Upon the wooden surface was a drawing of what might have been a snake.

The tradition was uniquely theirs, an arrangement between father and daughter, that went back almost two full years. For Ena Sheridan, all of five summers at the time, had decreed that it would be so. The girl, freckled and knock-kneed, every bit the most unfortunate bits of both her not uncomely parents, was nothing if not willful. And so it was that each time her father was set to ship out, Ena would choose for him, a creature of the sea. As per the rules of the tradition, the girl's father, who had something of a talent for scribbles, would then render said creature upon her bedroom door, always to the best of his ability and always in simple, white chalk. John would then promise to scour the waves and the nets, swearing not to rest until he laid actual eyes upon the chosen beast. In two years, they had already done the starfish, the octopus, the killer whale, three different types of shark and numerous seafaring birds. This last time, John had sailed North upon the Grey Lady, and little Ena had decided most surprisingly on a moray eel. Even now, he could remember feeling relief at that choice. With a name like the Grey

Lady, John Sheridan was afraid his daughter was going to finally ask for a mermaid.

Even in the dim, flickering light, John could see the chalk had been smudged on one side. But before he could move toward it, the faint voice of his wife reached him at last. The sound promptly filled his soul as if it were a pitcher--an empty one, made of a very thin sort of glass.

"Leave her be, John. She's sleeping'." Said Brona, as firmly as she was able. "The girl needs her rest. She's not been well."

"For God's sake, darling... what happened? I know Hodge has a knack for making whales out of minnows. Is that what this is? I can't stand it, woman! Talk to me, please!" The man sounded as if he were approaching frantic, yet for almost a full minute, his wife said nothing. His heart had begun to thunder outside of his chest. Fear seemed to be pulling it up into his jaw, where it meant to settle in his back teeth.

"Poor Hodge." When Brona finally spoke again, her voice was low and distant, detached somehow. "He's never really been the same, has he? After Catherine passed... well, it's almost as if he became someone else entirely." Just then, one of her arms tightened around the rag-doll--Ena's doll, as fingers absently ran through the yarn it had for hair. It was dark green, that hair. The color of of living seaweed, just like her darling girl had wanted. "Have you ever thought that, John. Same face, only dead inside." By this point the woman's words had trailed off so far as to be nearly unintelligible. John, already leaning in to hear them, placed a gentle hand on his wife's shoulder. But when she flinched and recoiled from the touch, he too pulled away.

"It happened on a Thursday." From somewhere, Brona's voice had found an edge. "Just two days after you shipped out. It was late morning. The air still had that golden smell. The sort you only get when summer's got one foot out the door."

She paused then, turning at last toward her husband, but not daring to connect with his eyes. Not those perfect sapphire eyes. They would be her undoing for sure.

"Anyway." She went on. "Being that it was Thursday, I was out back, hanging laundry. Ena and I had been at each other's throats all morning, though now, I can't recall what about. The usual nonsense I suppose. I know

I've never mentioned it before, but that girl is extra willful the first few days you're gone. Ena's little storms I call them. Usually I'm accustomed to the extra push back, but the fighting had started early that day and my head was throbbing like the devil. So finally, I gave in. I let her to go down to the shore to look for shells. I can remember yelling after her then, to mind the waves. Better not get your dress wet, I shouted. Not your pretty white dress."

"You let her go down there alone?" John immediately regretted the question.

"I certainly did not." Brona fired back. "The girl had wee Molly with her."

In that moment, heat flushed once more to the soft parts of her face, and Brona Sheridan dearly wished she could still cry. After a few moments, she muttered something into the tangle of green yarn. "Poor Molly Maeve... she lives between the waves... waiting for a little one, close enough to keep."

The pale woman inhaled sharply then, holding the breath. To her husband, it felt like a warning.

"I could see her every second. Out back, hanging laundry in the golden air. Every blessed second..." she pinched the bridge of her nose "except for the one that mattered. It was a freak gust of wind that did it. Blew the sheet right from my hand, carried it halfway down the drive. And the sheet itself, well that was our best piece of linen, wasn't it. The one with the little flowers you bought last Christmas. Seeing such a prize possession fly away like that, I took off like a fox after a rabbit. And as I ran, all I can remember thinking was how I was going to have to rewash the thing. About what a great tragedy and waste of good starch that would be." Brona smiled sadly then and said no more.

At this point, the pale woman took a deep, ragged breath--letting it out carefully, cautiously. John looked down to see that his wife's expression had changed dramatically. Brown eyes now glared unblinkingly into his.

There she is, he thought. *There's my darling.*

It was obvious that she was doing it on purpose. Starting the story too early. Taking her time working up to the only part that mattered. But the expression currently on her face, God, it was like she had aged twenty years in a matter of breaths. *Haunted*--that was the word that flickered across the brain of John Sheridan. And so he did not dare give voice to his frustrations. Whatever his family had been through, had been profound indeed.

"Please darling," He said at last. "Take your time."

At this, Brona pulled away. Once more turning her head back to the flickering logs. And though John couldn't see them, her eyes darted repeatedly from left to right, not staring at the flames, but reading them.

"I'm sure you'll be quite happy to hear that I wasted no good starch that day. As it happened, our best sheet landed quite gently, right on a dry patch of clover. After a couple good shakes, I had it back on the line. Even used an extra pin, just for good measure." Brona's body was racked by a sudden shudder, followed by an eerie stillness. "It was then that I realized I could no longer see our daughter."

The words were a poison dagger. Hearing them, John's muscles clenched. Chest, arms, stomach, neck... they were all fists now. He wanted to say something, but his voice felt very small. A tiny worm in a great, gaping cavern.

"Even as I ran, I shouted her name." Brona continued blandly. "I'm seven now, Mama. Big enough to look for shells by my own self. She'd been saying that for months, John. Seven years old. Practically a woman, grown."

Just then, John realized his wife was shaking. Not sobbing, but rather pantomiming the act. He reached out, but Brona flinched away, wiping phantom tears from her cheeks with the heels of too-thin hands. She turned once more to the doll, staring into its blue button eyes, or perhaps through them. And as she stroked the green yarn, the woman's voice came out thin and high--in the sing-song tones of a child. "Sweet Molly Maeve, she'll take you to her cave, and smother you with kisses, as salty as the deep."

"Brona." The word sounded feeble on John's tongue. "What - happened - to Ena?" Each word made its own demand.

"I don't know, John. I've already told you, I was chasing our good linen down the drive." Laughter bubbled up then, though it contained only misery.

Scowling, the large man seized his wife by the shoulders, lifting her to feet. "In God's name," His voice boomed like thunder. "What's happened to you, woman? Have you gone stark, raving--" But the question died upon his lips. In utter horror and shame, John opened his bear-paw hands. Though as the pale woman slumped back down, her joyless laughter continued to assault his mind. At that moment, John Sheridan had a terrible thought. He wondered if perhaps, the woman currently occupying his favorite chair--the woman who had once been the freckled girl down the way, pretty as a September morning, hadn't gone just a little mad. He reeled round, taking two forceful strides closer to the door marked with an eel, before he felt her hand on his shoulder.

The touch of a man's wife is something to cherish--especially after a long, lonely month at sea. But surely, this was the embrace of a specter, a living skeleton and John Sheridan recognized it not. He turned, locking eyes with the diminished creature that wore his wife's blue dress. And before another word could pass, she fell forward into his arms at long last. Brona buried her face down into the center of her husband's broad chest, breathing him in. Here was her favorite place in all the world. Only this.

"We scoured the shoreline, me and the Oistigan boy, Brian. It was he who first heard my screams. And before I knew what, Eamos Walsh came running with half of Barrowbrine at his heels." Her words were muffled, pressed as they were into her husband's natural bulk. "For almost a quarter hour, we looked, all of us screaming her name and wading waist deep in the muir. Back on shore, I had seen them, her little footprints were there, John. As was Molly." she gripped the doll tighter than ever "But nothing else. I swear to God, I only looked away for a heartbeat. Just one..."

At that moment, the woman was laid bare. Quivering and naked as any newborn babe. And like any babe in its first moments of life, Brona Sheridan did remember how to cry.

Possessing neither the will, nor the power to stop it, she gave herself over to the act, until her body convulsed in great heaving spasms. When the episode had mostly run its course, Brona looked up again to find that she was once more in her very favorite place. Wrapped in arms that could wrestle any sea monster to its grave. Without fear, she inclined her head to gaze into two perfect sapphire eyes. Though edged profoundly with pain, they still sparkled with indomitable, deathless love. Only this.

"Ena told me she knew better." The woman's words came amidst fractured breaths. "That she was old enough. Seven for God's own sake! Ena knew the waters down there were never fit for swimming. That the tide always flowed strange around our old bluff, and through those jutting rocks men call the banshee's teeth. Oh she knew, our little darling did."

Brona pulled away--staggering a single step back toward the hearth. When she reeled around there was flickering orange madness in her eyes.

"I can remember screaming." Said she. "Screaming for our little girl 'till water ran down my throat. After that, I could no longer separate the taste of drowning and that of my own tears. Each time someone pulled me out, I fought my way back in. She's out there, I told them. Just a little farther. By then, half of Barrowbrine was on the beach. Some stood waist deep beside me, hands cupped round their mouths, with our little girl's name on their breath. Others were diving into the muir to search the dark waters. I wanted to join them. Needed to. But they kept pulling me back. The bastards. I would have traded every one to get our sweet Ella back." Suddenly, all emotion drained from Brona's face. "But I had already made a trade that day. Our sweet daughter for a damned *bed sheet*. Our very best."

For an instant, John thought his wife was going to cry again, but she shut her eyes and shook her head, refusing the act.

"After a while--I can't say how long... I caught sight of old Hodge. The only man in the Barrow with enough sense to run away from the spectacle, and fetch a damn boat. I think, every eye on the beach was on him, then. All of us watched stupidly as his paddles slapped the waves, taking him nearer and nearer to the Banshee's pretty teeth. Hand to God, John, I never saw any man go so close to those rocks before." Brona shook her head, just as a shuddering breath forced its way past her lips. "Good old Hodge. If he had glanced over, I imagine we would have looked like a flock of geese, every neck stretched to see. Once he disappeared round the bluff, I felt again like I was drowning. Like there was salt between my teeth. Those moments were the longest of my entire life, John. Truth is, I'm not sure I remembered to breathe until I saw the tip of that little rowboat come back into view. And by God, there was something in there with him. Something little and wearing a dress. Still white, still pretty."

As John fell, his knees banged loudly on the floor. All of a sudden, he could hear his heart beating in his teeth. Absently he pressed a hand to his chest, though his wife seemed not to notice.

"Hit her head on a rock." Brona nodded. "That's what Doc Bartlett said later. Somehow, slipped, hit her head and was pulled out by the tide. Hodge had found her floating like a bit of driftwood, amidst the teeth. White as a ghost but face up, thank Christ."

"Face up?" John spoke warily. "Brona... is she really here?" His sapphire eyes were wet and gleaming. "Oh darling, that's all that matters! My God, you put the fear of the devil in me. I thought..." He pressed a little harder into his chest, working the left shoulder around in its socket. "Doesn't matter. My girl is safe."

Brona's expression was inscrutable.

"John. You need to let me finish."

The man said nothing. He simply didn't have the courage. Instead, he stared as a statue stares. Watching as his wife again turned to regard the doll in her arms.

"Ena had me make this three years ago. She thought wee Molly here would protect her from the real thing. Even insisted on the green hair." These last two words hung coldly in the air. "As all good children of Barrowbrine should well be, that daughter of ours was always transfixed by the rhyme. Took every word as gospel. But even at four, Ena was adept at wielding one word above all the rest--why. She feared the muir, but more than that, she yearned to know more of the bad lady who poisoned it. So, one night when you were away... I told her what I knew."

John flexed his fingers. Vaguely, he could feel an ominous pressure deep in his chest. Though it seemed to be swimming up veins in his left arm, he did his best to push the sensation away.

"According to my Nan," He could hear his wife say, "The creature in that rhyme was once a resident of our own Barrowbrine. Maeve Mcrue was her name, and the way Nan told it, she was quite the beauty. Blessed with shining green eyes and long, raven-hair... even if she was quite unable to speak. Despite this, the girl did swell before her sixteenth year. And though quite unmarried, young Maeve became the mother of not one squalling babe, but two. Twins she had, a boy and a girl. Both as healthy as they were beautiful. Nan said the father must have been a foreigner. Some faceless sailor with whom young Maeve had shared two days, and of course the one fateful night. For her sins, the young mother received no husband, only two hungry mouths--one for each breast. It was a fortunate thing that the girl's father was a decent man. He made sure that she and both her little ones lived well enough. For a time at least. Maybe it was the sun, or the summer's golden breeze."

Brona shrugged.

"However it happened, the idea of a picnic did occur to the girl. Of course, as with most days, Maeve's father was out catching supper. Surely he had warned her never to go down to that beach alone. She must have known the waters down there were never fit for swimming. But it is important to remember that while Maeve Mcrue was a loving mother, she was also very young. Maybe too young. Whether it was the little girl or her brother, Nan wasn't sure. After all, she had been no older than four herself when she watched the scene unfold--from her perch atop barrow's bluff. All she knew for sure was that one of the twins took one step too many. Maeve Mcrue watched a large wave took her child. Dragged it into oblivion. If she screamed as she ran, her calls were silent things. Even when the second child, followed their mum and sibling, there wasn't a soul in Barrowbrine who knew anything was but cups and roses, that fine summer day. Nan said, the young mother's life was over in a clap. I used to think that wasn't enough time for anything to be over. I really did."

Brona paused long enough to hug the doll, just as tight as she could.

"As it happened, that night, when Mr. Mcrue returned from sea, he found his daughter sitting on the front step. Her clothes were wet, and she was alone. He did his best to console her. To dry and warm and love her. But on the following morn, sweet, sad Maeve Mcrue did drown herself in the deep dark blue."

Brona met her husband's eyes then, just long enough to see the stark horror in them. To her, his skin looked off. Grey and clammy. Somehow, that felt fine, though. She was nearly done.

"Sometimes, it can be a hard thing. Separating the taste of the muir from that of your own tears. You see husband, Maeve Mcrue may have died, but she wasn't done grieving. And so it happened that the creature what lives off Barrowbrine's eastern shore, did come into being. No longer fair, nor young nor remotely human. The Mcrue girl had become a thing of salt and of spite-- seaweed sprouting where raven strands once grew. Poor Molly Maeve, she lives between the waves, waiting for a little one, close enough to keep. Sweet Molly Maeve, she'll take you to her cave. And smother you with kisses, as salty as the deep."

In that moment, John Sheridan realized that he was backing away from his wife. He needed to know what waited for him behind the eel-door. Ena's door. He needed that more than air.

"Leave her be, John. Didn't I tell you? Our little girl needs her rest."

The woman spoke softly, carried across the floor by pale feet. John tried to speak, but his throat felt dry. His arm, heavy and numb. It was difficult, but he managed to glance again at the door. It was a mere step away, now. Though smudged on one side, the eel was still a menacing site. He hadn't intended it to be that way, but when he had moved to erase and start over, Ena had cried out for him to stop.

"No, Da!" She had said. "I like it. It looks like it's singing."

"She adored those drawings of yours, you know. When you were gone, whatever beast you'd sworn to bring back stories of, seemed the only thing on her brain." As she said this, Brona appeared placid, but all too quickly, her expression returned to ice. "You should have been home, John. This, all of this, might well have been avoided, if you had only been home."

John Sheridan clutched harder at his chest. Breathing had become difficult and the numbness in his left arm was spreading. Sapphire eyes looked around, wildly. With his good hand, he fumbled at the simple rope handle. And as the door swung open, he watched as the darkened room was slowly revealed. John tried to breathe, tried to swallow, but his pounding heart had taken up residence at the base of his throat. God, his arm felt so heavy--almost as if it were made of stone. But he couldn't think about that. Right now, he needed light, needed to see inside his daughter's bedroom. On an end table stood a flickering oil lamp. Seizing the object, he brandished the light, pushing it into the darkened room.

John Sheridan made it nearly two full steps inside, before a powerful pain fired up his left arm and into his neck. It wasn't like before. All at once, the large man shot backwards as if he had been kicked by a mule. Promptly, the lamp shattered on the wooden floor, sending liquid flame into the air to splash the curtains. Screaming was impossible. Every ounce of strength was already being burned to merely stand and stare. Without looking at his wife, John Sheridan wet his lips, forcing his remaining energy into a single, burning question.

"What did you do?" His voice was far too small for a man of his size.

"Oh John. I've already told you." Said Brona Sheridan, pity hanging off her every word. "It was our very best bedsheet. The pretty one with the flowers."

The heat on the man's face was intense. An entire wall was in full blaze now, jumping from curtain, to table. It was heading straight for the girl's bed but for some reason, this fact was not nearly as vexing as what that bed contained. The thing possessed Ena's basic shape and size, but nothing more. There were no eyes, nor any semblance of a human face. Sleeping in the spot where Ena Sheridan should have been, lay a child-shaped silhouette rendered in uncountable grains of snow white salt. Sea salt. Only this.

"I told you to let me finish, John." Brona's voice sounded distant. Hollow. "What Hodge pulled from the muir looked very much like our Ena. It wore more than her dress, it had her face. Complete with my nose and your sapphire eyes. It fooled everyone but me. Only I could tell it was an empty thing. It wouldn't eat nor drink, and in four weeks, no word passed its lips. Day after day, I watched as the thing that wasn't our daughter wasted away. But last night I could stand it no longer. I knew the Ena-shaped thing wasn't really mine, but motherly instincts can only be denied for so long. So I forced it to have a drink. Just a sip of fresh water before bed."

By this point, John's face had contorted into a hideous mask. As his strength failed, his bulk slid against the wall and slowly down to the floor. Once there, the woman he had married leaned in to whisper. "There, there, husband. It'll be alright. You see, our Ena is still out there. She's with that witch, I know it. Molly Maeve paid for our little girl with a doll, you see? A thing she fashioned from salt and from spite. She was clever, leaving it for us to find like that. For us to pull out and fawn over, while she lead the real Ena Sheridan down to her house."

Brona smiled then, but it was a joyless thing.

"That witch doesn't know it, but I've seen her house. Every time I close my eyes, I can see that damn, glowing cave. That's where I hear her. She's been calling to me, John. Calling for her true mother. Awake I tend to forget, but I remember now."

To this, John offered no response. His shoulders had fallen still, utterly ceasing their subtle rise and fall. There were flames licking up his left arm, but

Brona paid these no mind. Instead she lowered her face to that of her dead husband, and placed a final kiss upon his cheek.

"You stay here and rest, John. Just rest. I have to fetch our little girl. To bring her home." At this, she permitted a shuddering sigh. "Ena will be so happy you're home."

The small cottage had become an inferno, though the pale woman never turned, never knew. Carried by gaunt bare feet, she padded down the cold path which led to the deep and the dark. When toes pierced the water, she hardly felt the cold. Though as her head dipped below the water's surface, Brona Sheridan did become distantly aware of a salty tang upon her lips. The taste was familiar, if somewhat difficult to place.

HIGH
FISHING

Night Fishing

There was an owl outside. It was calling out–asking the same thing over and over. Beckett wanted to call back to the bird. To give an answer good enough to make it stop. Unfortunately, the boy didn't know what to say. He didn't speak owl.

Unable to fight it off, a shiver traveled through the boy. The cold was real, but it was also a kind of fear. Beckett knew this because it was blowing from the dark outside and in through the open door next to his sister's seat. It was weird that Mommy had left it open like that.

When she left with Katie, Mommy had said not to worry. That she needed Beckett to sit tight and wait until she got back. He didn't understand why they couldn't all have gone together, but he wasn't about to argue. The last thing he wanted was for Mommy to get mad tonight. This was a special night. It felt like a birthday and Christmas all rolled all into one, because tonight, they were finally going fishing.

Earlier, when Mommy had woken him up, Beckett had been a little afraid. He'd thought that her eyes looked the way they did after a bad cry, but this was probably just the boy's imagination. After all, her voice had been extra sweet as she'd explained what they were going to do. After that, Beckett had felt silly for being afraid. Silly and very excited.

Daddy used to go night fishing all the time. Sometimes he would even be gone for a couple of days. Beckett used to ask if he could go too. The thought of standing out on the ice together, all bundled up under the moon seemed more than fun, it seemed like breaking the rules. Unfortunately, every time Beckett had asked, his father's response was always the same. He would laugh and shake his head–sometimes tousling his son's hair. For some reason Daddy liked going fishing alone.

Again, the voice of the owl cut through the boy's mind. Suddenly, the happy thoughts of fishing were forgotten and for a second, Beckett thought he might cry. Unlike Daddy, he didn't like doing anything alone. It was a very good thing that when they had left the house, he had remembered to bring Jake.

Lifting the stuffed bear, Beckett regarded his old friend. Then he pressed his face into the threadbare tummy and just breathed. In, then out again–over and over until the icy butterflies in his own tummy went away. Jake always made things better. He could chase away scary things and even make Beckett believe that things were going to be okay.

Back when he was new, Jake had smelled, very distinctly, of strawberries. Unfortunately, the strawberry air hadn't lasted very long. Beckett had asked Mommy if they could take Jake back to the store to make him smell right again, but she said that wasn't how it worked. To make matters worse, she had laughed at the question. Though Beckett hadn't protested, this had hurt. The boy didn't think the problem was very funny. Not one bit.

Now that both boy and bear were a little older and more mature, Beckett was faced with a hard truth. He remembered loving Jake's original smell and how safe it had made him feel, but the smell itself was fading like the details of a dream. Beckett didn't like that at all. In fact, the idea of losing the strawberry air was just about the scariest thing he could think of. It was for this very reason that the boy searched as he breathed. He was hoping to find one last lingering sweet-scented-whiff. He didn't need much. Just enough to remember.

Beckett held out his friend, checking the stitches in his tummy.

Jake was white-faced, dressed in pale pastels and covered in little balls that Mommy called pills. Beckett tossed Jake in the air, giggling as his friend performed an impressive aerial cartwheel. Among other things, Jake was a stunt bear. After a perfect landing, Beckett hugged the stuffed toy and inhaled.

As before, there was no hint of strawberries. Just the usual mixture of fabric softener, spilled juice and love. And that was okay too.

When the owl asked its question again, Beckett found that he wasn't so afraid as before. Brazenly, he slapped the window and proceeded to wipe away some of the fog there. Then, squinting through the glass, he checked the tree branches. Owls were hard to spot sometimes and even the little ones had very loud voices that traveled far. Still, he looked and searched until the window was foggy again.

Beckett frowned. The waiting was getting harder and colder.

Again, he looked to the open door. Katie's door. Beckett thought about unbuckling his seatbelt. About climbing across the seat and closing that door himself. Mommy had said to stay put, but she wouldn't mind... would she? Technically he wouldn't have gone anywhere. Just a quick trip to the other side of the car and back. The real problem was, in order to do that, Beckett was going to have to unbuckle himself. Something he was never ever supposed to do. It was hard to know what was going to make Mommy yell these days and Beckett didn't want that. He just wanted to go ice fishing. The way Daddy always did.

When they had left the house, Beckett had been so sleepy and things had gone so fast he'd completely forgotten to grab his jacket. Usually, when that sort of thing happened, Mommy would yell at him to go put it on, but she hadn't tonight. This was probably Katie's fault. Beckett's little sister was nine months old and she cried a lot. In fact, she had been doing just that when Mommy had shaken Beckett awake.

He remembered that now. Just like he remembered sitting at the kitchen table, trying to wake himself up. The room had been blurry and he'd had tried very hard to focus his thoughts. On the table was a baby bottle. Beckett remembered that too. It was the pink one with the yellow flowers and it was sitting next to something that felt very out of place. A container of tiny white circles had spilled out over the surface of the kitchen table. After wiping more sleep from his eyes, Beckett had realized that they were Mommy's pills. Even now he could picture how some of them were all smashed up. How those ones had looked exactly like sugar.

Beckett thought it was funny the way sometimes different things had the same name. Mommy's medicine and the little bumps on Jake were both called pills. That was funny.

"So funny I forgot to friggin' laugh."

Beckett shouted the line into the car's cold interior. It was something Daddy used to say. Back before he and Mommy were always mad at each other. Before Daddy left to start that new job in Ohio.

Staring at the fogged up window, Becket had to actively fight the urge to reach out. Not with a wiping hand, but with a drawing finger. Because every kid knew... when your window got like this, it was begging to be turned into a masterpiece. And, as it happened, Beckett was something of an artist. When he was little, loops and squiggly-lines were his style, but these days he was able to draw things that actually looked like what they were supposed to be. Other second graders he knew were pretty good at things like hearts, houses and trees, but none of them knew how to make a lobster.

Beckett liked lobsters. After Jake, they were probably his number one favorite animal. He always made a point to look at them when they went to the supermarket. They were in a big tank, right next to where you got the baloney. Beckett loved watching the lobsters–memorizing the different parts of their bodies so he could draw them better. Sure, sometimes the claws still looked like mittens, but he was getting pretty good.

Staring at the window, he released a small sigh. Aside from fishing, there was nothing in the world he wanted to do more than to draw a lobster, or maybe, an owl. His hand seemed to move by itself with one drawing finger extended. But before he felt the cold of the window touch his skin, Beckett stopped. Mommy hated when he drew on the windows like that. She said the oils on his finger made a friggin' mess.

As another shiver shot through the boy, Beckett put away his drawing finger. As much as he wanted to, he decided not to draw on the window. And so, with a resigned sigh, he put his drawing finger away and turned his attention back to Jake's tummy.

The owl was still out there. Still calling out its question to an unresponsive night. Beckett pulle Jake closer, sniffing, searching for strawberries, wishing the bird would just go away. And then he heard something else. Something that made him sit up straight.

Someone was coming.

"Mommy?" Beckett's voice was too small for anyone but Jake to hear, so he just listened. Devouring each slapping impact as the footsteps got louder, closer.

A face appeared in the window.

"Mommy!" He practically squealed.

The woman looked as if she hadn't slept in days. Her eyes were swollen. Rimmed with darkness and tears.

"Beckett. I thought I told you to drink your juice."

The boy looked over at the lidded sippy cup and his heart sank. It was still in the door's cup holder, still untouched. He had forgotten all about it.

"Oh," He said, picking it up. Quickly taking a pull of the orange juice. "Sorry, Mommy. I forgot. But I didn't draw on the window. See?"

"Yeah, baby. I see. Come on and unbuckle, okay?"

A smile bloomed as Beckett pressed his thumb into the square button. Like a snapped rubber band, the seat belt retracted and banged off the door.

"Okay!"

Though there was nothing wrong with his own door, the boy slid gleefully across the seat, towards his mother. He wanted to ask if she was okay, but... sometimes asking only made things worse.

"Mommy? Can I bring Jake?"

The woman was staring blankly in the direction of the pond. "I guess so, just... I need you to finish that juice for me. Can you do that?"

"Sure, Mommy." Beckett reached back into the car for his bear and cup. Not wanting to, he sucked some juice out of the spill-proof lid, wincing again at how oddly bitter it was. Then the two began to walk. The pond wasn't far. Just a short walk through the wooded path that connected it to the parking area. As he walked, Beckett wished for the second time that he hadn't forgotten his jacket. Now steadily shivering, he wrapped an arm around his mother's leg, trying in vain to siphon some warmth.

"Beckett." His mother pushed him away. "Stop it. Just drink your juice."

Crestfallen, he reluctantly took a series of long sips, until the cup was nearly empty. The further down the path they moved, the harder it was for the boy to recapture his original excitement. He knew he'd been wishing for what was about to happen, but the juice was making his stomach feel shitty. That was another thing Daddy used to say. Shitty. Beckett wasn't allowed to say that word, but it's exactly how he was starting to feel. Shitty and very, very sleepy. Of course he knew if Mommy knew any of this, Beckett would probably never see the pond again. So he said nothing–allowing for soft, crunching footfalls to be the only sound.

When the owl called out again, a strange thing happened. Beckett thought that he could almost understand what it was saying. That, funny enough, the bird's question was starting to sound a lot like one of his own. Something he still hadn't found the courage to ask.

Looking down at his mother's feet, the boy discovered that she had forgotten to wear something too. For one, brief instant, he had to stop himself from giggling. Walking out of the house without your jacket was one thing, but he had never forgotten his shoes before. He came very close to telling his mother how funny she was, but the owl's voice came again.

It didn't care about the woman's shoes.

"Mommy?"

No response.

"Where's all the fishing stuff?"

"Huh?" The woman sounded confused. As if she'd be roused from a particularly vivid dream.

"You know–the poles and... that thing that makes a hole in the ice?"

"Oh. Right. Yeah baby, I... brought all that before. Dropped it off on the ice."

Beckett tried very hard to picture Mommy taking stuff out of the trunk before she had left him waiting, but it's hard to think when you're very very tired, and Beckett was exactly that. Somehow more and more with each step.

A sudden lick of wind shot right through the boy, making him remember that he was not alone.

Unfortunately, Beckett found that Jake had gotten heavy. Even heavier than his feet felt. It took serious effort before the stuffed toy covered his face. The bear certainly wasn't better than his puffy red jacket, not by half–but like always, Jake managed to make things a little better. Still checking for strawberries, Beckett noticed where he was. Though they were out of the woods, the world had become little more than a freezing, blue-gray smear. He tried to focus, but it was too hard.

"Mommy... I'm too sleepy to go night fishing." That's what Beckett wanted to say. "Can we please just go home? I want to go to bed."

The woman was a few feet ahead. Standing there. Just there on the ice. Next to a fine looking hole and without any shoes. Through a series of long blinks, the boy could see that she was holding out a hand–beckoning for him to come closer. The thing was, Becket wasn't sure if he could manage another step. More than anything, he just wanted to lie down. To stop and let the cold have him.

The owl's question made Beckett's eyes shoot open. The jolt had rattled the bones in his chest. Almost enough to start him crying. Beckett looked up, hoping to see the dark shape of the bird at last, finding only the moon. And as he stared at the indistinct edges of that white circle, the owl called out once more. This time, the boy understood the question. He had gotten it wrong before. The bird didn't care about fishing poles or that thing that makes holes in the ice.

Beckett looked at his mother and noticed lines running down her face. One from the corner of each eye. These were ice, he realized. Frozen tears. Mommy was sad, but Beckett didn't have time to worry about that right now. The owl's question needed to be asked and he was going to have to translate it because Mommy didn't know how to talk to birds.

"Mommy?" Beckett's voice was small, but firm. "Where's Katie?"

At this, the woman flinched. The smile she offered was an unsettling broken thing, but possibly the truest expression the boy had ever seen.

"Close, baby. Real close." Carefully, Mommy sat down on the ice and slowly dipped her feet into the hole.

As she did this, the boy began to breathe frantically through his stuffed bear. In, out, in, out–each breath pulling him further down into the world of slumber and dream. Despite this, Beckett somehow knew that everything was going to be okay. That while he didn't always understand his parents, beside them was the safest place he could ever be. With this thought, the boy allowed himself to drift away--led by the reassuring warmth of a mother's hand and by the faintest hint of strawberries.

About the Creators

STEVE VAN SAMSON

is the author of "Mark of the Witchwyrm", "The Bone Eater King" and "Marrow Dust". A fierce proponent of character diversity & of avoiding cliché like the plague, his short stories have appeared in anthologies including "SLAY: Stories of the Vampire Noire", "More Lore From The Mythos" and in the comic series "Gore Shriek Resurrectus". Steve is also the co-host of the Retro Ridoctopus podcast and watches entirely too many black and white monster films.

DEREK ROOK

is a the brick-fisted maniac directly responsible for building the monolith that is Rough House Publishing. Having thrived in the indie horror comic scene for two decades, Derek has done it all. His bombastic art and writing can be found in killer works such as "Gore Shriek Resurrectus", "Halloween Returns To Haddonfield", Lucio Fulci's "Gates of Hell", among others. On the side, he continues to dispense his brand of vigilante justice in Worcester, Massachusetts.

For more information, roll up your sleeves and visit

www.roughhousepublishing.com